# LAW FIRM CONFIDENTIAL

## PEAR YONSEI

**CALUMET EDITIONS**

Minneapolis

**CALUMET
EDITIONS**

Minneapolis

SECOND EDITION DECEMBER 2022

10 9 8 7 6 5 4 3 2

Cover and interior design: Gary Lindberg

ISBN: 978-1-960250-01-8

# LAW FIRM
# CONFIDENTIAL

"Never forget that the best tools you have as a writer are yourself, your memories, your values, your POV or life perspective, your doubts, fears, and obsessions. Especially your doubts, fears, and obsessions! This alone makes your story unique. Write from yourself, not from what you think the market dictates. These stories take tremendous courage as they arise from your very soul. These stories will carry the power of the gods and result in universal, archetypal myths."

— *Catherine Ann Jones*

I dedicate this book to my many admirers in whose eyes
I could see the distant star that I was becoming.

## Acknowledgements

I'm grateful to the King County Library System for having the technological resources to accommodate the writing of this book. In addition, I'd like to thank all of those, who after reading the first few chapters, sat silent and said nothing—to me. Finally! I've perfected my technique and hushed the critics.

Writers Rock!

# CHAPTER ONE

## THE STORY

"Of course, there's every possibility this book
*could* finish me in the business."

~Anthony Bourdain, *Kitchen Confidential*

*By now, I was on the cusp of a new beginning. My sights were set on the Pacific Northwest. I wanted a fresh start. So, I began donating gently used clothes, shoes, and household items to Goodwill. As my apartment emptied out, a flood of memories and the realization of my very distant journey to the Pacific Northwest stared me stark in the face. Ready or not, my departure date was quickly approaching. In preparation, I printed two copies of MapQuest directions to bring along with me. I never use GPS devices when I travel, especially long-distance. I like knowing where I'm going instead of relying on a device to tell me too belatedly where to turn or merge.*

*The morning I departed from Texas, I packed the remainder of my belongings in my car, turned in my keys at the apartment leasing office and began my journey. I drove through my soon-to-be old neighborhood for the last time. It had been quite some time since I had traveled long-distance, but it all came back to me now. All I needed was endurance, stamina, and, of course, my gorilla grip glove to ensure my safety while traveling a journey of this magnitude.*

*Every day, until I reached the Pacific Northwest, was a lesson in how to navigate both familiar and unfamiliar terrain. I began my journey on I-35N—a familiar road I'd taken on day trips to Oklahoma. So, I felt confident driving I-35N to US Highway 287N from Boise City, Oklahoma, to US Highway 83N. But, let me tell you, these backroads are not for the faint of heart.*

\* \* \*

Like a hot-headed Mustang, I could take off running in any direction for no apparent reason. Yet, there was almost always an underlying reason. But you had to know me—*really know me*—to find out. You couldn't just get the inside scoop about me—at least *not from me*—living on the perimeter of my life. Burned too many times by disloyal friends, even family members, made me guarded, somewhat secretive about my movements. However, I had come up with a method of communicating my whereabouts. Inexpensive informants.

By March 2019, I'd evolved too much to remain in Dallas, Texas. Besides that, I'd gambled myself into a basement deficit playing the Daily Four lottery. Needless to say, it was time to go. My vice was kicking my ass. Not to mention, I was inundated with past due bills, which included unpaid toll fees. I was on the verge of becoming a scofflaw. Fortunately, I got out of town before my car was impounded.

Not that I was keeping it a secret, but I didn't disclose to anyone that my position as a Bankruptcy Paralegal had ended unexpectedly after three months. One of the partners had upped and moved to a new firm taking with her a bunch of big clients. I, on the other hand, was bound by a confidentiality agreement with my soon-to-be-former employer not to discuss the details of my departure from the firm. And, since part of that agreement was tied to my being paid, I didn't want to upset this arrangement by being vocal about it. Keep quiet. Get paid. That was my main objective—for now.

Mind you, I was allowed to continue working through the end of March, at which time my position would permanently end. Before that, I was quite comfortable living in Dallas, or so I thought. I enjoyed shopping for groceries at my neighborhood Wal-Mart, H-Mart and Sprouts; finding discount sales at Belk at the Galleria; and buying Merlots, chocolates and gourmet potato chips at World Market. I was content spending weekends being transported into INSP's world of classic westerns starring Clint Eastwood and watching re-run episodes of *Gunsmoke*, *The Virginian* and *Big Valley*. Little did I know, this alteration in my employment would re-pattern my life and rearrange it in ways I never anticipated. Twists and turns took me along pathways and roads I hadn't imagined exploring until a visceral desire drove me to parts unknown.

In the meantime, I continued going to work, searched Indeed.com and CareerBuilder.com for employment opportunities, and browsed law firm websites for job openings. After submitting my resume for several positions, I received an email reply from Lynn Beckett, the Human Resources Manager at Strobeck Keller, LLP—a law firm. As requested in her email, I called Ms. Beckett.

"Hello, Ms. Beckett. It's Paige Turner. I'm calling in response to your email."

"Hi, Paige. Yes, I received your resume and wanted to speak with you about a Floater Legal Assistant opening at our firm. Are you interested?"

"Yes, I'm interested."

Ms. Beckett provided a brief overview of the position then arranged an interview via Skype the following day.

My interview was scheduled for 2:00 pm. So, I left work around noon to be sure I'd have enough time to drive home, eat lunch, and prepare for the meeting. Since the leasing office in my apartment community had a business center, I reserved a computer for my interview—during which I met with Ms. Beckett. She explained the position in greater detail, provided some informational background on Strobeck Keller, and suggested I visit the firm's website. Then, Ms. Beckett introduced her boss, Alice Kaplan, the Director of Human Resources, who provided additional background on the firm and her role within the firm. I explained that my current position as Bankruptcy Paralegal would be terminated at the end of March, which is why I was looking for a new position. When my interview with Ms. Kaplan ended, Ms. Beckett returned to wrap-up the Skype meeting. She assured me that she'd get back in touch with me soon.

Two days later, while I was at work, I received an email and a voicemail from Ms. Beckett asking me to call her. So, I left my office, cell phone in hand, and took the elevator downstairs. It was sunny outside, but breezy. I stood near the building to shield myself from the wind. When I called Ms. Beckett, she offered me the position of Floater Legal Assistant. I accepted. We briefly discussed my start date, April 22, 2019, and other new hire details. Since I had to get back to work, Ms. Beckett informed me that she'd send my official offer letter to me in the mail along with additional paperwork I'd need to complete for a background check. I was elated that I found a new job before March ended. I wouldn't have to explain a gap in employment or bother to apply for unemployment benefits. It was only a matter of four weeks before I'd start my new job. But the job was three thousand miles away in the Pacific Northwest.

The good news: I'd receive a bonus from Strobeck Keller in the amount of two thousand dollars. The bad news: I wouldn't receive the bonus pay until my start date—April 22.

I was on a tight budget, but I managed to set aside some extra money for my long-distance move. It wasn't much. Heck, I wasn't even sure I'd have enough money for food, transportation and hotels. But I had to take that chance. I'd already accepted the job offer and Ms. Beckett was expecting me to start work on April 22.

Before I left Texas, I sent the following email:

Dear Friends,
After seven years in Dallas, it's time for a change. I'm relocating to the Pacific Northwest. I look forward to exciting times visiting the Northwest coastlines of Coos Bay and Rockaway Bay, embracing new adventures, and meeting new friends.

All my best,
Paige Turner

Long before I ventured to Dallas, Texas, I started my law firm career as a Floater Legal Secretary at Dewey Kingsbury LLP, a law firm in Washington, DC. It wasn't easy. The daily demand was to meet high expectations under pressure. There were external challenges and internal demands. But for all its concomitant pressures, I liked working there. It had its benefits.

Dewey Kingsbury provided me an opportunity to gain valuable experience as well as earn a great salary. The firm also offered a competitive benefits package that included health and life insurances, profit sharing and 401(k) retirement plans, short- and long-term disability coverages, and flex spending and health savings accounts. As an employee, I took advantage of these benefits by enrolling in health insurance and other benefit plans offered to employees by the firm.

This top-notch DC firm paid me rewarding bonuses and lucrative raises. I was well-liked. And, the majority of the perks I received—free parking, free dinners, and such—were due in part to the graveyard (5:30 pm to 1:30 am) shift I worked. So, the powers that be made sure I was well taken care of—considering.

Some of my co-workers were like a second family to me. In fact, when I won fifteen thousand dollars in the lottery, I vacationed in Cancun with Bonita, a co-worker, for four days, including my birthday. I had a lot of friends that were mad at me for taking Bonita, especially since we were casual friends and I hadn't known her for very long. But from the start, I felt comfortable in this work setting. It was one in which I was appreciated. Attorneys and staff were civil and always addressed me by name.

I recall one evening arriving at work wearing a brown mini-skirt suit. My supervisor, Rosalind, saw me as I exited the elevator heading for my workstation and asked, "Paige, what are you doing?"

"Being young," I replied.

Everyone in the lobby laughed. So, I was free to be me. Being around attorneys, in this law firm somewhat influenced me to behave like them. By that, I mean I dressed like them, spoke like them, and was on occasion mistaken for them.

Caroline, an associate attorney, told me that a conference call was delayed with a client because the client was trying to reach me by phone to conference me into the call. When Mr. Kramer asked his client, "Who are we waiting on to join the call?" Caroline said Mr. Kramer's client responded, "Paige Turner." Mr. Kramer then asked Samuel, his client, "Why are you trying to reach my evening secretary?" Everyone on the conference call laughed.

To some extent, I over-identified with my job at Dewey Kingsbury. One time, before reporting to work, I had eaten something that gave me a bad case of gas. I couldn't stand up without bending over. An ambulance was called. When I arrived at the hospital, I was diagnosed and given a G.I. cocktail. I didn't like hospitals and was eager to leave. I kept asking when I would be discharged. "Not yet," the nurse told me again. Then, after five hours, I was finally cleared to leave. In haste, behind an emergency-room curtain, I started dressing. The next thing I knew, I was being wheel-chaired down a hall in a head-restraint contraption. I had passed out and may have hit my head while getting dressed to leave the hospital. Now, the nurse was taking me to get a CAT scan. When I came to, my first concern was that the people who saw me in my helpless condition had no idea that I worked at Dewey Kingsbury.

The Washington, DC, office consisted of twelve floors of attorneys that practiced areas of law such as bankruptcy, energy, public law and policy, white-collar crime, entertainment, and private equity to which I reported on a daily, as-needed basis. Most attorneys already had a nine to five assistant. My tasks consisted of picking up where first-shift legal secretaries left off, handling overflow work, and completing overtime assignments for attorneys whose watch was almost always on billable time.

My daily tasks were no walk in the park. Assignments ranged from inputting an entire month of billable time for eight attorneys in the Belgium office (prior to the 9:00 pm EST deadline) due to a power outage there, to updating heavily edited transactional documents that required deciphering penmanship that looked like chicken scratch to transcribing tapes about campaign finance contributions to stuffing holiday envelopes for a regal attorney, Sylvia Dozier.

Sylvia dressed with professional flair. So, can you imagine when staff saw her walking towards me with two Neiman Marcus shopping bags downstairs in the lobby? They assumed Sylvia brought gifts for me. I let their imaginations run wild with envy as I disappeared with Sylvia into the elevator, where she handed me the shopping bags and informed me of my assignment for the evening.

My job was mostly driven by time constraints. So, after glue-sticking photos of Sylvia's family to more than five hundred holiday cards, I packed the sealed envelopes back in the same high-end shopping bags to deliver to Sylvia's house in upper Northwest near Embassy Row.

Sylvia answered my knock at the door and welcomed me in. Straightaway, I exclaimed, "Sylvia, your house is beautiful!"

"Isn't it," she replied.

I wasn't surprised by her confident candor. It was typical Sylvia Dozier. She was always in agreement with compliments. Sylvia was "ALL OF THAT!" She was also married to a partner attorney. She drove an eighty-thousand-dollar Jaguar and was respected and well-connected to exclusive DC circles. The mention of Sylvia Dozier's name secured reservations at posh restaurants, which I discovered upon dialing up *The Palm*.

When I reported back to Sylvia that *The Palm* was completely booked, she asked, "Did you tell them it was me?"

"No," I replied.

Her response was silence. So, without any prodding, I called *The Palm* again. This time, I requested a reservation for Sylvia Dozier. *It worked!*

As I wrapped up the details of Sylvia's reservation, she called out to me, "Did I get in?"

"Yes," I replied.

Now we both knew she pulled rank, and that's the way Sylvia liked it.

Whenever staff thought I was behaving above my authority, they would look at me and ask facetiously, "Who do you think you are, Sylvia Dozier?" Then, we'd laugh uproariously in unison at the *thought* of me trying to emulate Sylvia.

I spent a lot of time assisting Sylvia with personal administrative matters and got to know her quite well. As a result, Sylvia felt comfortable calling me from her car.

On a very cold winter day, Sylvia called and asked me to meet her downstairs to pick up handwritten time entries. In a hurry, I rushed outside without my coat. Shivering, I walked briskly towards Sylvia's Jag. As I approached, Sylvia let down the driver's side window. She told me that the Metro bus behind her had rear-ended her and asked me to walk around her car to take a look to see how bad it was. There was barely a scratch.

Meanwhile, the Metro bus incident resulted in the offloading of all of the passengers at the height of rush hour. Sylvia sat snug in her plush heated seat, innocently oblivious to the disruption she caused these commuters. While the commuters, now huddled at a nearby bus stop, glared at Sylvia through her expensive windshield as she refreshed her makeup on this bone-chillingly cold evening. They couldn't imagine how the now out-of-service Metro bus had put a dent in Sylvia's plans that evening. They lived worlds apart.

* * *

Warren Kramer, an attorney in the firm's energy practice group, frequently asked his assistant,
Maureen, to arrange for me to assist him with
overtime assignments, which mainly consisted of
making revisions to voluminous transactional documents with handwritten edits that extended into
the margins around the edges of pages, including
inserted pages with additional edits continued on
the back of pages. It could get road-mappy, but
I had the wherewithal to follow Mr. Kramer's
thoughts on paper. Come to think of it, I never
knew his astrological sign. We just worked well
together. So, I began assisting Mr. Kramer with
increased frequency, especially after Maureen discovered I could interpret his scribble.

Most evenings, I spent a great deal of time at
Maureen's desk revising documents for Mr. Kramer.
Sometimes, Mr. Kramer's son Eli would call to talk
to him, tell him what's for dinner, and ask when he
was coming home. Mr. Kramer almost always told
Eli that he would be home soon. Shortly thereafter,
Mr. Kramer would gather his belongings, give final
instructions, and leave the office for the evening. I
followed Mr. Kramer's instructions to the letter,
which included working with associates in the energy group to finalize revisions to documents, faxing
final copies to clients once approved, and emailing
Mr. Kramer a copy of the same.

As time progressed, I became more involved
in Mr. Kramer's practice. At some point, he con-

tacted Human Resources and requested that my title be changed to *Evening Legal Secretary to Warren Kramer*. I had no idea until Maureen made me aware of it on the firm's telephone directory. I was designated Mr. Kramer's point of contact for clients calling after business hours. This caused quite a stir among attorneys that also needed floater assistance. It upset Doug Markham, a white-collar crime defense attorney, to the point that he became vocal about it.

One evening, Doug approached me while I was sitting at Maureen's desk and asked, "What am I supposed to do if I need evening assistance and you're working for him?"

"There's another evening floater, Naija," I responded.

"Isn't she primarily assigned to Vladamir Sokolov?"

"I'm not sure," I replied. "But you're welcome to call Human Resources. I'm sure someone there will see to it that you get floater coverage."

In a seriously annoyed tone, Doug asked, "What is it that you do for him anyway besides ordering dinner?" He went on venting his frustration while Mr. Kramer was on a conference call in his office closing a deal with a client.

Mr. Kramer was not very well-liked at the firm, and many of his peers said as much to me. It was probably because I worked directly with Mr. Kramer that many of them told me how they felt. However,

Mr. Kramer stayed busy with his clients. It was difficult to detect if he knew or even cared about what others thought of him. He was oblivious to the whispering criticism that permeated the office. He had the savvy ability to rise above it. He didn't acknowledge it; therefore, it didn't exist.

From my observation, what mattered most to Mr. Kramer was his family and his clients, not chaotic comments swirling about him at the office. So, like Mr. Kramer, I tuned out the critics. But, as usual, someone always reminded me of the Kramer-haters. This time, it was Mr. Kramer's own secretary, Maureen. In hindsight, I can't really blame her. She was just trying to give me a fair warning.

On my way to an assignment one evening, Maureen called me aside and asked in a whispery tone, "Who are you working for tonight?"

"Lester Royse," I answered. "Why?"

"I called HR to get you to work for Warren and was told you had already been assigned elsewhere," Maureen said.

"Just so you know," Maureen added, "Lester and Warren don't get along, so please do not mention Warren's name while you're working with him."

"All right," I said agreeably without particular concern over my shoulder as I proceeded down the hall to my assignment for the evening.

Brenda, Mr. Royse's assistant, greeted me when I arrived at her desk and explained the assignment I'd be working on that evening.

"Mr. Royse is in his office on a conference call," said Brenda. "But he will come out from time to time and give you pages to revise." Then Brenda left for the evening. It wasn't long before Mr. Royse stepped out of his office.

"Hi, Paige!" Mr. Royse said exuberantly.

"Hi, Mr. Royse," I replied. "You're quite lively today."

To that, Mr. Royse responded, "Are you a Redskins fan?"

"Yes," I said.

Mr. Royse proceeded to tell me all about his day at the Redskins game.

"I've gone to games before," Mr. Royse told me, "but I've never been as wild as I was at yesterday's game!"

"I was yelling and cheering and shouting! I mean, I was REALLY into it!" said Mr. Royse. He was as demonstrative as his voice was excited.

"It sounds like you had a great time," I said.

"I did!" said Mr. Royce. "I had a really great time."

Still high on the energy from yesterday's football game, Mr. Roysc, a middle-aged man, worked with renewed enthusiasm. He went back into his office after handing me some edited pages to revise and resumed what was beginning to turn into a marathon conference call.

Sometime later, Mr. Royse bolted out of his office with a document for me to fax to a number he scrawled on a post-it-note. Before disappearing back into his office, he asked me, "Do you know where the fax machine is?"

"Yes, Mr. Royse," I responded. "It's the fax machine across from Mr. Kramer's office." *Uh-oh,* I recalled Maureen's warning after my blunder.

Mr. Royse slammed his office door closed. Then, he snatched open the door just enough for me to see his angry bulging eyeballs. In a snarly voice, he said, "That is NOT Kramer's fax machine! It belongs to the Energy Group!" Mr. Royse slammed his door again, this time as if to shut me out of his world.

The next day, I told Maureen about the incident.

"I had no idea the slight mention of Mr. Kramer would strike such an angry chord in Mr. Royse," I said. "He frightened me."

"I tried to tell you," Maureen admonished.

We laughed about it, but while doing so, I was still somewhat rattled by Mr. Royse's reaction last evening.

I didn't like arguments or angry people, and for good reason. Once, I got into an argument on Labor Day. After about two months, I was still feeling the negative reverberations from that argument. That awful experience taught me to avoid arguments, and angry people. They siphon too much energy. So, I steer clear of both.

By far, Sylvia and Mr. Kramer weren't the easiest attorneys to work for at Dewey Kingsbury. Their preferences required a certain degree of adaptability and flexibility. The fact that Sylvia and Mr. Kramer called on me consistently for support, I'd like to think that I met their standards, which enabled me to work so compatibly with them.

I could see myself building a long-term career at this firm. However, I quickly learned, it's a man's world, but even so, I still own my own pussy.

# CHAPTER TWO

"Impressions in the present are often colored
by memory images that may appear at the
most unexpected moments."

~Frances E. Vaughn, *Awakening Intuition*

*For me, driving 287N at night was like diving into the
Pacific Ocean with a pod of Orcas and never being
attacked. Like I-76W, at night, this road is so dark.
I could barely see ahead of me. As I drove further
along, it fogged up as temperatures dropped, and the
night's cold set in. Again, it was just my eyesight, my
headlights, and, most importantly, God protecting
me. Focus was also key! The darkness made me feel
isolated. It was overwhelming! What convinced me
to take such a risk? The lure was a right-pointing
arrow on a sign towards Denver as I approached
287N—a lone, two-way road—bridging Oklahoma*

*and Colorado. Truth be told, I wanted to wake up in Colorado in the morning. Besides, at night, there was less traffic to contend with, not as scary as seeing wide-load mega-trucks hurtling towards me even at controlled high speeds in broad daylight. While the mental tension associated with driving this back-road any time of day or night had a propensity to cause back spasms, I loved and lived for these "High Life" moments.*

*Before turning that corner (a u-turn after the fact would be a death wish), I shifted into reverse gear, backed up, and took another look at the sign to be sure I wanted to go on instead of staying the night in Boise City, Oklahoma—a short distance ahead. And, with as much nerve as it would take to dive into the Pacific Ocean, I proceeded into a fog of famil-iar, yet unknown darkness. With the exception of an occasional glow of massive eighteen-wheelers con-fronting me at high speeds, the surrounding darkness made me feel as if I was out of my natural element. But much road respect to the poised drivers of these eighteen-wheelers. They unswervingly held their own lane. Professional drivers. God bless them! The darkness on this backroad was punishing.*

*I had been driving since 9:45 am. And aside from an occasional reprieve from the road, I had been in go-mode for the past twelve hours. I reached Lamar, Colorado, around 10:45 pm and checked into a not too fancy hotel. Driving the last one hundred miles or so on this very dark road had me so focused*

*I couldn't sleep. At first, when I closed my eyes, I could still see a glow reminiscent of eighteen-wheelers in the rearview mirror of my mind. I slept with the lights on.*

*"Yes, there are alternate routes to Colorado," I wrote, ending one of my signature travel stories—Pictures That Tell a Story—I later sent to friends via email touting: "It's funBNme!!! But that's not why you're reading this story. You want to know what it's like to live The High Life.*

\* \* \*

I never felt a need to compete. Beauty was a forerunner.

Mine was a kind of beauty that waited until puberty to blossom. Sure, there were glimpses of its latent qualities hidden behind my eyes and in my body, germinating its own unique characteristics of recognition within me, genetic coding that held specific measurements—the equidistant jewels embedded in my pubescent breast, the girth of my hips, thighs, curvaceous waistline. The core of my femininity awaited the orchestration of Mother Nature to set my biological clock in motion at the appointed time to unleash my very own youthful brand of womanhood upon the Earth.

As a grown-ass woman, I hadn't intended to be a seducer of men. But whatever antenna I had up was attracting professional, good-looking men with sexually voracious appetites. Their pursuit was relentless.

Reggie was six-feet, two-inches tall, brown-skin, and bald with a full-bodied muscular physique. He was the epitome of the Bee Gee's description of "a woman's man"—always suited up and on the move. But Reggie made time to talk to me. And whenever we talked, I could sense seduction pulsating through his pores and, although he wore a wedding ring, I could tell it would take more than one woman to hold *him* down—*unless it was me*. Obviously, I wasn't his woman, so there was no need to ponder the thought any further until he showed up at my desk one evening.

After fixing the computer problem, Reggie stayed a while. We chatted about me, him and work. He asked, "Why aren't you married?"

"The right man hasn't asked me yet," I told Reggie. "Honestly?" I continued, "I think marriage is an exercise in how much bullshit you can take off someone else, including the children the union produces. I've had my share of babysitting jobs since I was twelve years old and wanted none of it! No changing diapers, nursing babies crying to my face, or any other responsibilities that go along with married life. The only dreams I want to fulfill are my own. "Mine," I said, "will be a footloose and fancy-free lifestyle. My ultimate goal is to *stay* care-free—at least until I meet a man who can give me the lifestyle I *really* want."

"And what's that?" Reggie asked.

"The High Life," I replied. "I'm talking 'Jordan to the Max' lush life." My head was full of dreams.

In spite of my rant, our conversation ended on a cordial note. Then, I got back to work.

I'm sure Reggie could see, if he had not already sensed, that I was a high maintenance B.I.T.C.H. (Babe in Total Control of Herself).[1] My wardrobe consisted mostly of high-end designer clothing: Kay Unger suits, Lois Hill jewelry, Via Spiga shoes, and bad-ass Guess sunglasses. I observed the effect my image had on people. Like the time I was introduced to a co-worker that responded by saying, "You *sooooo* have my stamp of approval." As she looked me over, her eyes landed with recognition on the charm of my Lois Hill necklace. Once, a guy almost fell off his bicycle when he saw me wearing Guess sunshades with metallic silver lenses. When I pulled up at gas stations, men paid to gas up my car and pumped it, too. Women befriended me. I got lots of attention. And, it wasn't because of the designer stuff I wore, either. The way I carried myself told people how to treat me—*with nothing less than the utmost respect.* And I got it.

A few days later, Reggie stopped by my desk. We got into a conversation about relationships again. It gravitated toward the topic of sex. I could tell his interest was piqued, so I teased him a little. Our conversation ventured into unchartered territory, and before I knew it, Reggie showed me a pic of his raw man-piece on his phone.

Reggie made it abundantly clear that he intended to have a sexual relationship with me. I was young, curious, and wanted to explore his feelings for me. So, I strung him along.

I told Reggie I would be off work on my birthday. Almost immediately, he insisted on coming to see me. I considered. Hmmm. Playing with sexual fire was risky. But my nature felt naughty, so I extended Reggie an invitation.

I answered the door fully dressed and invited him inside. I could tell Reggie arrived at my place with preconceived fantasies. I'm sure he was hoping I would be scantily clad waiting for him to do whatever he wanted to me. Instead, we talked. He wanted to touch me, feel me and kiss me. Now that we were alone together, I wondered why I let Reggie come over in the first place. While we sat on the sofa together, I saw him for who he truly was—an irresistibly sexy man that belonged to another woman.

Reggie kept reaching for me, pulling me, telling me to come closer to him, but my detached manner put some distance between us. Finally, he said, "Come here." Reggie hugged me close to him. He could tell I wasn't ready. He was gentle, understanding, caring. I kissed him back. He asked me to put on something sexy for him. I turned on the sound system and disappeared into my *boudoir*.

I reappeared almost naked, wearing a thinly laced black teddy with stilettos. I watched Reggie's composure unravel.

*"Damn, girl!"* he exclaimed.

The classic love song "Chances Are" was playing in the background. He grabbed his crotch, unzipped his pants, and pulled his penis out, massaging it while glaring at me. He made me feel powerful because I held the key to something he wanted. I waggled my pelvis in front of him. By now, Reggie was laid out on the carpet. I stood above him with my buttocks facing him and bent over so he could look up my ass and see the fissure of my freshly waxed pussy. *This* enticed him to an extreme. Reggie did a lot of skin slapping, nipple-sucking, and clit-rubbing. After branding my image of womanliness on his brain, he begged to fuck me. I refused.

He left, looking dejected.

*Hmpff!!* Reggie was a big dude. I had to pull out my pussy whip on that mutha-fucka.

\* \* \*

I hadn't been to church in a long time. It was a non-denominational evangelical church, where the Pastor preached damnation to the soul of fornicators, adulterers and the like. I felt uneasy about going back to visit and sitting amongst the congregation but decided it was time.

During my visit, Sister Dorothy, who notoriously carried a bottle of holy oil, stopped me and asked, "Where have you been? Have you found a new church home?"

"Yes." I wanted to respond amusingly. "I *have* found a new church home. Its name is Reggie, where

I worship regularly on my knees, mastering the art of fellatio."

While I didn't reiterate my exact thoughts to Sister Dorothy, I did, however, tell her that I was involved with a married man. To that, Sister Dorothy responded, "I'm going to pray for you, baby." As Sister Dorothy started to open her bottle of holy oil, I told her I didn't plan to attend altar call for prayer and asked her not to anoint my head with oil, because nine out of ten, I would still be fucking—*oops!*—still messing with this married man. "I don't want to play make pretend—*not with God*," I said. So, Sister Dorothy honored my request.

*Yaaaass!* By now, Reggie had conquered my pussy and planted his victory flag on it. I wasn't proud of having an affair with a married man, *but the things he did to me and how* made me stick with him like a stamp on a postcard. So, in spite of the circumstances, I dug in my heels, got back in the saddle, and let Reggie ride me like a jockey in the high stakes Preakness.

Things became hot and heavy between us. Although I told Reggie I wasn't very good at it, he asked me to get on my knees. "I like watching you suck my dick," he said. Reggie sweated profusely whenever we made love. I enjoyed getting slippery wet with him inside me and writhed in pure pleasure beneath his buff body.

Reggie was good about letting me know his whereabouts. One day, he told me he was going on a family vacation, and I wouldn't see him for a week. I missed him.

When Reggie returned and came over to my place, I appeared wearing a short sheer gown. "Something in My Heart" played on the sound system. He barely made it through my front door before I pounced on him, unzipped his pants, and pulled his penis out, inserting it between my glossed lips like a chocolate-covered banana. I sucked it salaciously like a Charms blow pop. I plunged his penis deep in my mouth—up and down. Then, I crowned his head with an unforgettable tongue swirl that made Reggie breathe rhythmically, as he breathlessly called out to me, *"Damn, baby!"*

By now, our involvement became consensually intense. For days, after frolicking with Reggie, I could feel the pressure of his groin still on my pussy.

Our game of seduction had graduated into a full-fledged affair. We went on a love-making excursion. Reggie loved tasting my pussy juice. So, I let him eat me out as often as he liked—*even at work*. Yes. We fucked *at* the office, *in* his office, I serviced him in the server room, and I let him lick between my in-betweens. Reggie relished putting his face in my pussy. And I absolutely, unapologetically carried on with this incredibly sexy married man.

I'm not sure *what* Reggie told wifey, and I didn't care. All I knew, Reggie was with me most of the time and paid my bills.

I wasn't the usual mistress. I didn't beg Reggie to leave his wife or nag him to spend time with me. He wanted to. And, he spent most of his free time with me. When he wasn't with me, he missed me and called me. I was my own woman, and Reggie knew that. However, I admit, I did love him.

But let's be candid here. Men really only look for what they're not getting at home. For instance, if a man feels unappreciated, unloved or misunderstood, he searches for fulfillment elsewhere, which leads some women to believe that men are dogs. This may or may not be true. Even so, you have to know how to keep *your* dog at home.

A case in point, growing up our bodacious barking German Shepherd, Radar, was so big and bad that he sometimes walked himself. At 2:00 am every morning, my mother put a white T-shirt on Radar and let him out of the house. He always returned home at 5:00 am that same morning. Not once did a stranger or neighbor, for that matter, knock on our door to bring Radar home. Neither did we find Radar staying at anyone else's house. You get what I'm sayin'.

However awkward it was, Reggie was there for me. He even attended and stayed the night with me after my grandfather's funeral, during which quite a few women, who had seen Reggie talking to me, asked me who he was. With nonchalance, I told them, "He's just a friend." With all kinds of comments of approval, with added emphasis, some of the ladies let me know what they thought of Reggie and that *"he had it going on."* I knew where I stood with Reggie, but I thought to myself, *"Don't let me fuck a bitch up in here!"* Even two of my sisters approached me at the funeral asking about Reggie. "Too bad he's married," one of them said. I ignored that comment and stood my grieving ground at my grandfather's home going. My sisters knew I was too much of a "good girl" growing up to get involved with a married man. I managed to keep my virginity until I was almost twenty years old. So, no one—*not even my own mother*—could fathom the idea of *me* being involved with a married man—*not now*.

One day after entering the office building, a woman approached me walking at a brisk pace that mysteriously slowed down as she got closer to me. Her focus stayed on me. She looked in awe at me from a short distance, then walked right up to me and asked point-blank, "Are you fucking my husband?"

I looked at her questionably. She said, "Reggie?"

Her eyes swept over my perky breasts in my summer dress. I looked at her then at the security guard in the lobby. I saw the anger soften in her eyes momentarily. She said, "You're very beautiful." Then, she walked away. I never told Reggie about my encounter with his wife. Thankfully, I was holding the Ace of Spades!

About two years into fooling around with Reggie, I started realizing that I didn't want my main squeeze to be a married man. So, I told him we couldn't see each other anymore. Reggie acted out of character. I experienced all sorts of dramatic encounters with him when I removed my pussy from our "friendship." What bothered Reggie most was that I dropped him on a whim without warning. Our conversations, once endearing, now escalated into arguments, which I walked away from many times. I was experiencing a moral awakening. It became stronger than my passion for Reggie. So, I left the firm.

My phone was a smoking gun, unloading rounds of incessant worries and remorseless pain, shattering the silence of pre-dawn hours, leaving my heart spasmodic, fear-hemorrhaging. It was another dream chasing me.

I was lying to myself if I thought leaving that firm would curb my contact with Reggie. I couldn't seem to get off the married-go-round. He continued calling me all hours of the day and night, trying to smooth talk his way into my heart again. He invited me to lunch. We laughed and talked like old times when we first met. Before parting ways, Reggie kissed me on the lips—in public. I melted like butter.

Reggie's dick was a hard hurdle to jump. I kept falling and landing on it, but Reggie made it hurt so good.

As Teena Marie crooned on the radio. . .

You made love to me like fire and rain
Ooh, you know you've got to be a hurricane
Killing me with kisses oh, so subtly
You make love forever, baby
You make love forever

I ain't gonna let you go that easy
You've got to say you love me too
I ain't gonna let you go that easy
I'm gonna give it all to you
Portuguese love

Reggie made my bed rock.

I honestly didn't know if I would ever get over Reggie so I tried not to think beyond this moment. We just fucked phenomenally. My feelings fluctuated. We couldn't keep our hands off each other. We had no immediate plans to stop fucking with each other. My bedsheets were saturated with Reggie's sweat. Too tired to do anything else, we threw some towels on the bed, cuddled, and went to sleep.

# CHAPTER THREE

## The Favored One

"Have you ever banked on luck? Yes! I have
bankrolled on it."

~Pear Yonsei

*At some point, I must have drifted off to sleep be-*
*cause I woke up to a sunny but cool morning. As the*
*day progressed, it became cloudier. It took a while*
*to reach Denver, but for now, I was happy just to be*
*back in Colorado.*

*After miles of even more focused driving on this*
*two-way backroad, I merged onto I-70W and headed*
*for Denver. I could have taken I-70W to E470, exit-*
*ed 289 toward Fort Collins, and merged onto I-25S*
*then crossed into Wyoming, but I wanted to visit my*

*old stomping grounds in Denver. But first, I got grid-locked in early afternoon traffic. While sitting in my car, in my own lane waiting for traffic to move, an eighteen-wheeler passing by in the left lane popped a rock off one of its tires that struck and cracked my windshield.*

*I counted down the remaining miles to Denver. Within a fifty-two-mile radius, I pulled over on the shoulder of I-70W to take a snapshot of a road sign indicating that I was twelve miles outside of Byers, Colorado. I-70W was a familiar Interstate that I'd driven on frequently during my "High Life" travels. I recalled memories of Denver days past when I fun-binged and sent postcards to friends that read: "Living elsewhere is a half-life, not The High Life!"*

\* \* \*

My grandfather, Edward Earl, was a card-playing gambler. At the age of twelve, I asked him to teach me to play Tonk. And, he did.

Learning how to play this card game empowered me. I recalled feeling this same sense of empowerment when I saw *The Wizard of Oz* for the first time as a young girl. I was impressed with Dorothy from Kansas and believed that I held the key to wherever I wanted to go in life. All I needed was the right pair of sparkly red shoes with which to click my heels and, I too would be magically transported to a wonderland of my own where all *my* dreams would come true.

Growing up, whenever I faced a hurdle of impossibility, I asked myself, *Why can't I?* In time, I found that the combined knowledge of these two very powerful impressions became a useful and dangerous formula for everyday living. But I never planned to live an average life. I made above-average grades, have above average looks, and I intended to live an above-average life. *I'm so vain!* And Richard, my grandfather (my grandmother's second husband before I was born), blamed himself for spoiling me rotten that way. So there, I was off the hook.

Richard bought my first car—a granite gray Honda Civic. He gave me Neiman Marcus and Macy's credit cards in his name to use for shopping, and he frequently gave me money. During my shopping sprees, I bought a ninety-seven-dollar blouse and a one hundred-and-sixty-seven dollar dress. I was a self-admitted cash-burner. My interpretation of QuickBooks was based on how fast I could book a flight on Expedia. com. Still, I hated when Richard cornered me on the telephone with questions about my purchases on his credit card statements. But he wouldn't stay mad at me for long. I was the daughter he always wanted but never had with my grandmother.

I wasn't the baby, the eldest or the middle child. I was the favorite. And, as siblings, we all knew that Richard gave Katie the money to buy our Christmas gifts, but Richard made a point of calling me out separately at Christmastime to bestow a single gift from him to me. It was specially wrapped by Richard.

Every Christmas, when we visited our Grandma Katie's house, Richard would walk out from his bedroom in sock-covered feet, past the kitchen, and into the living room where we all sat watching a movie—usually a western—and in dramatic fashion, he'd call out to me: *"Weenie!"* (a nickname my mother gave me). I would jump to my feet and stand at attention as if I was about to be presented with a medal of honor. Then Richard, extending his gift-bearing hand, would recite his annual two-word ceremony: *"Merry Christmas!"*

I appreciate Richard for taking the time to buy a gift for me, personally wrap it, and present it to me. It made me feel important. However, I could tell that Richard's ostentatious display of gift-giving inflamed my sisters. As I stood up to receive my gift from him, I could see daggers of envy in my sister's eyes. At first, I felt bad for them. But when they behaved jealously about it, I told them, "This is *exactly* why Richard doesn't buy gifts for any of you at Christmastime." I beat them over the head with Richard's preference for me, especially when we got into tit-for-tat disagreements. It really got under their skin. Then, they would run to Mother. But she ignored their jealous tattling. I was *her* favorite, too. So there, like the Berlin Wall, I had a fortress around me. *"No weapon formed against me—"*

But, one night Richard died in his sleep. . . . *OH MY GOD!* And my old world of privilege seemed to pass away with him.

As the top-most branches of my family tree were pruned, arguments escalated. I could still hear the boom-box effect of their voices reverberating off the walls. Screaming at the top of their lungs—trying to over-talk each other—as if anyone would suddenly be convinced of the others' truth. It was then that I realized Richard never told me no. He bought whatever I wanted. As this realization set in, I wondered, *Who will take care of me now?*

My uncles claimed they couldn't find the New York Life insurance policy Richard had me sign as sole beneficiary nine years prior. My head swirled with grief and confusion. During the days leading up to Richard's funeral, my uncle called me, demanding the pin number to Richard's bank card. I knew it but declined to give it to him.

"You can't withdraw money from Richard's bank account," I told my uncle. "He's deceased! You need to contact the Social Security Administration and let them know that your father recently passed away to stop the monthly SSI deposits to Richard's bank account." Threateningly, my uncle responded, "The Social Security Administration will have to catch me running and shoot me in the back to get back their money." At that moment, I wondered what danger might come to me if I didn't give my uncle the pin number to Richard's bank card. My uncle made angry accusations against me that intensified when he found one of Richard's cigar boxes full of cashed checks that were written out to me.

I'd been born into a family of professional arguers; none of them lawyers, mind you. But they had the uncanny capacity to argue each other under a table. When some family members' behavior got too strange and caused me to resort to vengeful, retaliatory talk, Richard would reiterate a familiar refrain in broken English from his hometown in Louisa, Virginia: *"Baby, it don't worth it."* It was Richard's way of saying, *without really saying it*, that I had to take the "high road." Well, I had done that all my life up to this point! Richard was gone now. My life was under a new world order: *Weenie-ism.* I had tolerated some shit off my family while Richard was around that I would now not put up with. So, without Richard around anymore, I decided *I'm going to do what the fuck I want to do!* Even if it meant I'd become the worst kind of Aquarius—*a rebellious one.*

I'd been the caregiver for three of my grandparents since I was fourteen years old. It began when my grandfather, Edward Earl, tried to commit suicide. I was probably around twelve or thirteen-years-old at the time. My mother took us to visit Edward Earl, as she often did, and to my surprise, a spot on the living room carpet was bare. I made a big deal about it. My mother shushed me. "We will talk about it when we leave."

"Dad," my mother later explained to me, "tried to commit suicide by slitting his throat. He's been dwelling too much on the past living alone." Now, I recalled Edward Earl's occasional apologies to my mother for not buying her a pair of Chuck Taylor tennis shoes when she was a teenager. He felt badly about it now that he was aging. He thought up things to worry about. I could see how living alone at his age was beginning to affect him. He needed nurturing and some form of companionship. "So, I've decided," my mother said, "to let Dad come live with us." That was great news to me!

My mother signed Edward Earl up to attend a senior citizen community center so he could participate in daily activities while she went to work, and we went to school. My responsibilities included making breakfast for him—eggs, bacon, grits, and Taster's Choice coffee. I sometimes sat at the table and had a cup of coffee with him, which made me feel like a grown-up.

We talked about all sorts of things before I left for school. I learned about his family history, why he moved to Washington, DC, from Raleigh, North Carolina, and how he met my grandmother, Katie.

Edward Earl's "senior citizen bus," as my sisters and I referred to it, drop him off around the same time as our school bus. My mother assigned me the duty of preparing meals for him. This was an honor for me because it gave me time to sit and talk with Edward Earl and get to know how he actually lived his life. Maybe it would give me some insight into—without directly asking—why he had tried to commit suicide.

Anything that kept Edward Earl alive was fine by me. The fear of death taking anyone in my family was an unbearable thought for me to consider, even at my young age. Besides, I thought, Edward Earl was too handsome to end his life tragically like that. "Wouldn't he miss seeing me," I thought as I talked with him. Living at the house with us made Edward Earl feel included, like part of the family again.

Edward Earl smoked Kool cigarettes. When he moved into our four-bedroom, two-bath home, he was smoking a pack a day. Whenever the ice cream truck bell rang, my sisters and I knew Edward Earl would ask one of us to get him a pack of cigarettes. Without my mother's knowledge, my sisters and I charged Edward Earl twenty-five cents to run this errand. So, if we were playing outdoors when the ice cream truck bell sounded, all of us would make a beeline to the house to see who could get the money from Edward Earl to buy his pack of cigarettes.

Edward Earl was highly regarded. And, whenever he took us anywhere with him—even to the corner convenience store to buy a box of Frosted Flakes for breakfast—I stood proudly when he introduced us as his granddaughters. People looked at us with admiration when we accompanied Edward Earl.

Sometimes, during our weekend visits at Edward Earl's home—before he moved in with us—he would get a phone call. After the call, he would get up and get dressed. As we prepared to leave the house, Edward Earl put on one of his cool hats—which he never left the house without—and took us along with him to card games. We played upstairs with other children while he gambled downstairs. I admired and appreciated Edward Earl in many ways, especially after I learned more about his life during our coffee conversations.

Edward Earl had gotten sick several times before his health completely failed him, but often pulled through and was usually back at home in a couple of days wearing one of his cool hats during his usual evening strolls while smoking a cigarette. Young boys in our neighborhood respected him and told me and my sisters that they thought he was cool. What impressed me most about Edward Earl was his innate dignity. Whenever I look at photographs of him now, I can see this characteristic in his person-ality. He wore his dignity like one of his cool hats.

Some years later, Edward Earl had undergone a surgery that didn't go so well. It seemed to cause his health to further decline, and when his stitches burst in the middle of the night, it was my mother who found him the next morning almost on his deathbed. She went into emergency mode and called an ambu-lance. I was too distraught to go to school. I stayed home and cried myself into the worst headache, not knowing if Edward Earl would live to see another day. My mother warned me that things didn't look good.

How could she remain so calm? And where was the rest of the family—Edward Earl's other children? It just so happened that my mother stayed home from work that day. Otherwise, I would have been the one to find Edward Earl in that awful condition. "You would not have known what to do," she said. "That's why I have to put Dad in a nursing home." *OH MY GOD! What?*

My mother didn't want to do it, but it would have been too much on her to take care of Edward Earl and us, too. She endured a significant amount of backlash from her siblings about her decision. But they offered no assistance with his care, only criticism.

Almost every weekend, my mother took us to visit Edward Earl at the nursing home. Then, I noticed our weekend family visits slacked off. Outside interest took precedent, and about a month or so later, we paid Edward Earl a visit. He had lost a significant amount of weight and had a tube in his throat. I asked my mother, "What happened to Dad?" She said he was losing weight because there weren't enough nurses at the facility to feed him. *Oh yeah?*

By now, I was in tenth grade. I was having none of that bullshit nonsense. Edward Earl was the grandfather who helped my mother with our upbringing, cut watermelon for us into special triangular slices, gave us coffee and spearmint flavored ice cream, and most of all because Edward Earl was my grandfather and a big part of my world growing up.

I began using my school tokens to take two buses to the nursing home weekdays after school to feed Edward Earl his dinner. I intended for him to get well and come back home to live with us.

When one of the nurses spotted me in Edward Earl's room, she asked, "Who are you?" With matter-of-factness, I introduced myself as Edward Earl's granddaughter. Further, I said, "Y'all need to do something. My grandfather is not accustomed to living like this. He comes from a loving family, and my mother put him here to be taken care of. You have got to do your job!" When I arrived home around 7:00 pm, I told my mother I went to visit Edward Earl at the nursing home. I never told her about what I said to a nurse there. But after my visit, someone from the nursing home called my mother on a regular basis to let her know how Edward Earl was doing.

\* \* \*

"Katie," my mother said, "was a party girl." She loved going to cabarets. When she died, it took me eight consecutive Saturdays to clean out her closets full of party clothes. I didn't want to leave this painstaking task to her husband, Richard. I'm sure he was grief-stricken, as was I, since I had been Katie's caregiver after she had a stroke and fell down in the house while Richard was at work. After her fall, Katie lost the use of the left side of her body because she refused to do the physical therapy required to recover her mobility. "It was too painful," Katie told me. So, she let her health decline. Having been a party girl, I think it was more painful for Katie to see herself in a partially handicapped condition than anything else.

Katie looked like a movie star. And, I was glad when people recognized her features in me. Whenever I visited Katie at the hospital, a nurse would say, "That's Katie Henderson's granddaughter!" The nurses were always happy to see that I took the time to visit with Katie after work. Visiting with Katie was important to me, because I wanted her to know that I cared. The nurses also took good care of her.

When we were kids, Katie bought fabric and made our summer clothes on her sewing machine. I remember her visiting us at home unpacking bags with short sets with matching tops and sundresses with all kinds of colorful patterns. Katie made some of these outfits for herself and wore them whenever she took us on picnics or playtime before her health declined. Katie even made my mother a pair of culottes with exotic zebra and leopard print fabric. She gave us some freedoms that my mother didn't allow. We could be our carefree selves with her and talk easily—that's what I remember and appreciated most about Katie. She was also frank to an alarming degree.

I recall going on a day trip with Richard and Katie one summer to Richard's hometown of Louisa, Virginia. On the way back home, we stopped at a beach. Katie got out of the car, rolled up her pant legs, and walked along the beach to feel the coolness of the water and the sand between her toes. "It sure is nice out here," she said. After a while, Katie let Richard know that it was time to go and asked him to stop at Ruff 'N' Ready Crab House on the way home to get a dozen Blue crabs. *Oh, joy!* When we got home and walked inside, Katie kicked off her shoes and said, "I've never seen so many ugly people in one place in my life." *"Grandma!"* I exclaimed.

Even in her wheelchair-bound condition, I got her all dolled-up like pictures I saw from her cabaret days. I colored Katie's hair copper red, applied her lipstick, and got her dressed up for Richard when he came home from work some weekends. Richard always paused when he entered the house, admired the youthful beauty in Katie's eyes, and kissed her on her lips.

Now that Richard was gone, I'd have to make my own way in life. And the way I knew best to supplement my nine-to-five was fun but risky. However, if I got skilled enough, I could probably make it work.

# CHAPTER FOUR

## Ego in the Spotlight

*"It's not necessary for anyone else to under-
stand the story of your life but you."*
*~Pear Yonsei*

It seemed, wherever I worked, someone was always trying to taste-test my pussy. And, my ego knew how to give it to Dré Skarsgaard good, like a porn star would. In fact, he called me his private porn star and paid me good for it, too.

Dré was a good-looking man. He reminded me of the classic movie star Charlton Heston. Dré was an antitrust attorney and fluent in four languages: German, English, French and Spanish. He worked with my boss, JR, who was blond with engaging blue eyes and a commanding voice. He was a subtle flirt. We all had been playing fantasy sex for a while before any transaction took place. It began when JR pranked me with an electric chewing gum toy. The shock from JR's toy made me call out his name in such a way that I attracted the attention of the secretaries sitting nearby. One of them, Tabitha, rushed over to find out what was the matter with me. I told her about JR's prank.

"Girl," Tabitha said, "he doesn't play with *anyone* like *that*. He must like you."

I shrugged and laughed.

"Paige, how old are you, anyway?" Tabitha asked.

"Why?" I said.

"Just asking," Tabitha said and walked away.

Before JR's prank, each morning when he arrived, he locked eyes with me and held his gaze until he was out of sight in his office. I talked to my friend, Becca, about it. She asked, "Does he look good?"

"You'll have to come up here and see for yourself," I said.

Becca and I had been friends since we met at the University of Maryland in a course on African Studies. Becca was Haitian. So, we studied French together as well.

Since Becca's workday ended half an hour earlier than mine, she came over to my office. When JR finally came out of his office, I introduced him to Becca as I prepared to leave for the day. They shook hands and had a brief exchange. As we headed for the door, Becca asked, "How can you work with him around?" she whispered. "He's so sexy."

Becca and I hung out frequently after work. We met up at a designated spot, usually, at my office, the Metro Station or her house. Depending on the subject matter of events that transpired during our workday, we went to one of three places: Starbuck's to discuss things that ticked us off over a raspberry Frappuccino with whip cream and fudge drizzle, The Cheesecake Factory for candid chats while eating good food that made us forget what we were mad about in the first place or to simply shake it off, and Borders Books to browse the mind, body, spirit aisle to find the latest publications on that subject since our last visit.

One time, Becca and I had dinner at The Cheese-cake Factory for an entire week, during which we cut-up, belly-laughing so hard about stuff that happened at work and elsewhere that we thought for sure we would get thrown out of the restaurant. Going to The Cheesecake Factory was our time to let our hair down, sit back and talk about anything on our minds. As we did, other patrons were sometimes drawn into our conversations. Some of them even paid our tab. I remember one time, Becca and I were having dinner and engaged in a very involved conversation when a waiter appeared and interrupted us for what felt like the umpteenth time. Annoyed, I half-exploded, "*What is it*?" He said, "Those people over there," pointing to a table, "asked me to give this twenty-dollar-off coupon to you and your friend." Becca and I thanked the waiter and the patrons, then resumed our conversation.

Sometimes, Becca and I met up just to vent, and then we headed to one of our favorite spots for the evening, including Chipotle, where female servers stared enviously at us and Cloud Club, where we drank Mojitos, met new friends and danced. Besides hanging out after work, Becca and I attended a Constituent Breakfast on Capitol Hill, where we had our photographs taken with former President Barack Obama and Senator Richard Durbin.

Becca worked for a real estate company and invited me to a party her bosses threw at The Mayflower Hotel. We, of course, dressed to the nines for this event. Becca wore a black and white spaghetti strap gown revealing much of her double-D cleavage that got plenty of attention. I wore an aquamarine silk Kay Unger evening dress that had a diamond broach just below my cleavage. Becca knew how much I loved Kay Unger clothing, so she bought this dress for me at $150 off the clearance rack at Mahmoud's boutique in downtown DC.

The party's theme was Las Vegas. There were card gambling tables, slot machines and Powerball ticket giveaways. We had a FABULOUS time taking pictures, drinking wine and gambling. After the fun had been had, the following week, Becca and I emailed pictures of The Mayflower event to our friends. Some of them thought we'd actually gone to Vegas.

Becca and I painted the town this way almost every weekend, especially in the summertime—attending flashy events, snapping it up, and emailing pictures of ourselves to friends hyping that we were somewhere having a fabulous time. We had a lot of fun times together. Becca was a Leo and loved the spotlight. As her opposite polarity—Aquarius—I tended to gravitate towards the opposite end of the spectrum. It was probably best that way. Our egos would never collide.

Since Becca and I always hung out together, it was not unusual for me to invite Becca to my firm's fiftieth-anniversary celebration. That's how Becca met Dré, and we all became friends. I introduced Dré to Becca and left them to chat while I mingled with co-workers.

When I returned, Becca, Dré and his dad were sitting at a table engaged in conversation. I joined them and shook hands with Mr. Skarsgaard and introduced myself. Immediately, I noticed Dré's facial structure resembled his father's. Dré told me his dad was visiting from Germany and asked me, "What would you like to drink?"

"A Cosmopolitan," I replied.

The four of us chatted for a long time and were the last to leave the firm's celebration. Before parting ways, Becca invited Dré to join us for a cultural event at the Haitian Embassy the following week. He agreed.

A week later, Dré drove us to the Haitian Embassy. As we toured the embassy, we browsed and admired the artwork. Becca introduced us to some of her associates, including the ambassador to Haiti.

When Sabreena, one of Becca's good friends, introduced herself to me, we shook hands. Just as Dré was about to exchange greetings with Sabreena, she said, "I'm sorry, Paige, I didn't catch your last name." Before I could respond, Dré blurted out, "Rosenstein, maybe." Becca and I were astonished, to say the least. Then, I responded to Sabreena, reintroducing myself, "I'm Paige Turner. It's nice to meet you, Sabreena," I said.

After meeting several artists while browsing and admiring their work, it was getting late, and Dré told us he had to get home to walk his dogs. So, we left for the evening. When we arrived at Dré's house, he offered us a drink, Becca and I chatted with Dré briefly, then we left.

Becca couldn't wait to talk about Dré's comment to Sabreena earlier that evening.

"Why would Dré suggest that your last name might be the same as JR's?" Becca asked me. "I don't know," I said. "This has to be something they have talked about." Becca speculated. "How could he just come up with that on the fly?" asked Becca.

"This is wild," I said.

One morning I was running late for work and emailed JR from my personal email account to let him know. Shortly after that, I started receiving emails from JR to my personal email letting me know of his whereabouts. Right away, I let JR know that he had reached my personal email and asked him to use the office email address instead. But it happened again.

One time, he was right there in his office, and I was at my desk when I noticed he had sent another email to my personal email account, this time, regarding a work-related matter. I went into his office and told him that he reached my personal email account again. As before, JR promised to be more mindful when sending emails to me. But it happened again.

So, taking JR for the prankster he was, I initiated an email to him from my personal email letting him know that I liked him, too. When I arrived at work the next day, everything appeared to be fine. JR said nothing to me about my email to him. The next thing I know, around two o'clock that afternoon, I was called into Human Resources by Abigail, a prudish old bitch whose sexual fire had obviously extinguished, and placed me on administrative leave with pay until further notice. Two days later, Abigail called to tell me I was fired.

When I told Becca about it, she blew her lid! "What the fuck! First, Diana hired you because you're attractive, now Abigail fired you for doing the same thing JR did to you? That's a double-standard, Paige!" Later that evening, we met at Starbucks to discuss the firing in greater detail.

After analyzing the firing top to bottom, Becca planned a fun-filled weekend to make me feel better. We went to the Cloud Club, took pictures, had some drinks, and danced until we were tired. On Sunday, while shopping, Becca bought a crystal picture frame. In it, she put a picture of us from the club and bought a bottle of wine to give to Dré as a surprise since he started hanging out with us after work some evenings.

First thing Monday morning, without scheduling an appointment, I arrived at a legal placement agency, where I had once won a five-hundred-dollar prize for making the most referrals. So, I was confident that I would receive an assignment right away. And I did. But when the recruiter asked me, "What happened to your seventy-thousand-dollar-a-year job?" I wasn't prepared to answer. It was embarrassing. Flummoxed, I offered a nebulous, indirect response.

That evening, Becca called to tell me that she met up with Dré to give him the picture of us in the crystal frame and the bottle of Pinot Grigio. "Dré asked about you," Becca said. "I broke the news to him about what happened with JR and that you got fired." Alarmingly, Becca added, "Paige, you are not going to believe that we almost got into an accident." *"What?"* I exclaimed. "Girl, yes!" Becca continued. "Do you know Dré got so distracted and almost ran up on a curb?" said Becca. *"What!"* I exclaimed again. "He was like, you mean Paige isn't my co-worker anymore? That's when I knew," Becca said, tellingly, "that Dré likes you."

\* \* \*

I worked a long-term temp assignment for a few months. During that time, Dré and I got acquainted.

We talked on the phone, and he invited me over to his place. After a drink or two and chatting, Dré excused himself and went upstairs. He returned butterball naked! I was shocked!

"You know I look good," he said.

Like the bone structure in his face, Dré's body was chiseled, and his ego was definitely in the spotlight. I turned away from him. He pulled up on me, put one hand around my waist and the other down my pants with his fingers on my pussy. We were now on the floor of his living room in a wrestler's stance. "Dré," I said calmly, "get off me." It was kind of comical seeing him behave like this considering his professional demeanor at the office. Dré was an aggressive type. He knew what he wanted and went after me. I asked Dré to get dressed so I could leave. I didn't want to open the door while his nakedness was exposed. He stepped aside, and I left his house.

Dré called me the next day, apologizing for his behavior. He said he shouldn't have come on so strong and asked if I would come over to see him. I did. While we sat on the sofa in his living room having a drink, Dré asked, "Why did you come back?"

"Maybe, I liked what I saw," I said.

Dré took me on a tour of his house. We walked through the living room to the kitchen, where he opened the door to show me the backyard. Then, we climbed the stairs and entered his office where a balcony overlooked the backyard. The bathroom was immaculate and masculine, and finally, his bedroom.

I stood at the threshold of the door. "I can see it from here," I said. But Dré wanted me to come inside.

He pulled me close to his body. With both his hands on my ass, he kissed me. He told me he wanted me then and there. "Dré," I said. "This is not a good time of the month." He told me his preference. I told him mine. He wrote me a check for eight hundred dollars. Dré undressed. Then, I got down to the business.

Call it what you want, but if you think I was a trick, you're wrong. I was his high-prized fantasy—a magician of sorts. I could make both our dreams come true at the same time. And, at least I had finally got off the married-go-round.

Dré watched me work my magic, while his facial expressions and deep breathing let me know just how much he liked the way I sucked his pork sword. I could see the passion ignited in his eyes.

Dré picked me up frequently from work for lunchtime *rendezvous* and to spend time with him. We walked his dogs, had dinner and drinks, and watched TV. But most of all, we enjoyed fucking each other's brains out. Dré often joked, "You can't stop two people from fucking if they goin' fuck." I thought Dré was making silly fuck-talk. That is, until he asked me to marry him and move to Germany. But for reasons of my own, I just couldn't.

* * *

When my baby sister, Monica got pregnant at the age of fifteen, I made it my business to find a second job while I continued working as a floater legal secretary from 5:30 pm to 1:30 am to ensure that she finished high school and to prevent her from becoming a welfare mom. If I had anything to do with the upbringing of Monica and my nephew, neither of them would consume government assistance food such as powdered eggs or use evaporated milk to eat cereal. I had had enough of that in my own upbringing.

There was a DC bitch that hibernated inside me from way back when we used to live in a project community in Southeast DC called Valley Green on Wheeler Road. Valley Green was so bad it was torn down before I grew up. By then, we'd already moved to our four-bedroom two-bathroom home. Originally, we were Northwest Washingtonians; that's where we were born—so making the transition from a vibrant neighborhood in Northwest DC to a project ghetto in Southeast DC like Valley Green was a frightful three-year experience for me. I remember a teenage boy, Jean, stealing my bag of candy and having to say "excuse me" to a neighbor's dog to get a crowd of people on the front porch to move aside so I could take out the trash. When I got back inside our apartment, I told my mother.

My mother, Ms. Prunie, had a way of fixing things that I couldn't possibly imagine. So now, I was able to play safely outside roller skating, jumping rope and hopscotch. Things always worked out for the good with my mother around. Yet, the growing pains of living in Valley Green had left a negative imprint on my mind. People who lived there were always ready to joust or fight. One day, my mother told us to go outside and play while she got ready to take us to a movie. Instead, after a short while playing outdoors, we ended up taking my sister, Harriet, to an emergency room, because a boy in the neighborhood threw a brick that hit her on the temple. Harriet ran inside the house with the side of her face bleeding and crying to our mother. I knew then and there that no one in Valley Green would ever hurt me because if they tried, I would protect myself at all costs. But by the time I was nine years old, my mother moved us away from Valley Green. I wondered if it had something to do with the fact that I stabbed a boy in the neighborhood with a discarded dope needle I saw lying on the ground. After that incident, my mother took me to get a tetanus shot, and that was the end of Valley Green as we knew it.

When I began to develop a figure at twelve years old, my mother told boys in our neighborhood, "I will take a baseball bat to your head if you mess with my daughter." One time at the community swimming pool, a man looked at me in my bikini. I heard my mother's voice reverberating throughout the pool area, "Get your eyes off my daughter. She's only sixteen-years-old." My mother protected me. So, I thought I was doing the same by helping out Monica when she got pregnant.

Instead, I caught a lot of resentment from family, especially my other sisters, for helping Monica during her pregnancy. But I told them, "I'll be damned if she has four grown sisters, and not one of us reaches back to help her!" If there was anything I learned from my mother and my grandparents, it was you didn't abandon people in a time of need. So, Monica and I went through her pregnancy together. I was there as much as I could be during Monica's pregnancy, but most of the time I worked temp assignments from 8:30 am to 5:00 pm, then went to my evening full-time job from 5:30 pm to 1:30 am.

I gave Monica two hundred and fifty dollars every two weeks so she could support herself during her pregnancy while going to school. When my nephew was born, I took on a full-time permanent day job in addition to my evening full-time job to pay for my nephew's daycare expense, which was six hundred dollars a month. But I kept running into friends and church members that told me Monica was going around saying bad things about me.

While Monica didn't appreciate the sacrifice I made to support her and my newborn nephew, Naija, another evening floater I'd worked with at Dewey Kingsbury, was so inspired by my initiative that she also took on a full-time day job to better support her own family. She was married and expecting her sixth child. After about a year or so, Monica obtained a government voucher that paid for my nephew's childcare expenses. So, I quit working two jobs.

\* \* \*

As a result of working temp assignments, I knew how to navigate the law firm terrain in DC better than most head-hunters that tried to recruit me. So, the recruiter that placed me on the long-term temp assignment after the JR fiasco was not surprised when I told her I found my own full-time permanent job.

In my new position, I worked as a floater legal secretary. I worked a daytime shift and volunteered to work overtime as needed, which occurred quite often. At first, I assisted the intellectual property group, and then I was moved to a workstation in the franchise practice group. Judy was my new bay-mate.

As I got settled in at my new workstation, I took a moment to look at myself in a compact mirror and put on some lipstick and gloss. When I turned around, I noticed Judy looking at me with her tongue practically hanging out of her mouth. She was sizing me up. *For what?* I didn't know.

Judy was a mature, but fun-loving woman who loved listening to the radio and would break out in a demonstrative karaoke sing-along with songs that played on her radio at any given moment during the workday. Yvonne, the secretary that sat on the other side of Judy, would laugh along with Judy and me whenever Judy did that. Judy was the life of the party.

One evening while working late, Judy's boss, James Garfinkle, came over to my desk and said, "If you keep working overtime, you're going to be one rich bitch." We laughed heartily together. From that point on, whenever James came out of his office to speak with Judy about any work-related matters, he almost always stopped at my desk to talk to me. James was tall, blonde and solidly built. He had strikingly vibrant eyes. Occasionally, James told Judy where he was going when he left the office. Whenever he told Judy he was on his way to the bank, she jokingly remarked, "Bring me back a couple thousand, okay." Then, they'd laugh as James walked down the hall.

Judy sometimes overheard me making plans to meet up with Becca after work to go to The Cheesecake Factory or to Pam's Nails for a mani-pedi and eyebrow wax. On one particular day, Becca and I were meeting up to go to a new club. Becca told me that she was bringing a friend, a new guy she recently met. When my call with Becca ended, Judy asked where we were going. "A new club on Connecticut Avenue," I told Judy. She looked at me with an intrigued stare and then said, *"Have fun!"*

The next day during my lunch hour, I went to CVS to pick up the developed pictures from the club event the prior evening. Becca and I always took a disposable camera with us whenever we attended events and got photo prints and electronic copies. When I returned to my desk, Judy came over to my workstation. I told her I had pictures from the club event. She was excited to finally see Becca in the photos. "She's cute! Now, I know who you're hanging out with." Judy said. As we continued looking at the pictures together, I'd forgotten that I had some pictures of myself in a bikini in that roll of film.

When Judy saw my bikini pictures, she took a few of them and ran away from me into James's office and closed the door.

In the weeks to follow, James came on strong. He walked up to my desk and asked how I was doing. "You wore that blouse so I could see your boobs while I'm talking to you," James said, laughing.

Later that week, James invited me to Proof, an upscale restaurant, where bottles of wine run upwards of three thousand dollars. We went there a couple of times. The first time, a paralegal who sat near my workstation, overheard James making plans with me to go there and she pretty much invited herself. So, she came with us. James liked to drink Grey Goose Vodka with an olive or a lime twist. I asked James what made him choose the olive versus the lime or vice versa. He said, "It depends on the type of day I'm having."

One evening as I was gathering my belongings to leave for the day, James came out of his office with his suit jacket in hand and walked down the hall with me. We left the office together in his Lexus from the garage.

James drove to a posh restaurant on K Street, where he had his car valet parked. We proceeded upstairs, where a waitress seated us at a table, took our drink orders and left us to browse the menu. James made light conversation. While I was responding, he reached over the table and planted a kiss on my lips. When the waitress returned with our drinks, I ordered seared salmon with rice pilaf. James ordered a crab cake with fries and another Grey Goose with an olive. Absorbed in conversation, we hadn't noticed the crowd growing around us since entering the restaurant earlier until I excused myself to go to the ladies' room. I didn't know where the ladies' room was, so James said he would show me.

As the restaurant's speakers thumped with Pussycat Doll lyrics. . .

> I'm telling you to loosen up my buttons, baby (uh-huh)
> But you keep fronting (uh)
> Saying what you going to do to me (uh huh)
> But I ain't seen nothing (uh)

I opened the door to an elegant one-room stall with James close in tow. Once inside, he locked the door and undid his pants. His cock thrust forward like a delicious sausage inviting pleasure. As my head moved back and forth the length of it, James moaned deep with satisfaction. While James ran his fingers through my hair, my mouth stroked his cock. Aroused, his dick-pulse quickened. I stood up. He pulled up my skirt, opened my blouse, and sucked my bouffant boobs. Then he went down on me. "I love the way your pussy tastes," James told me.

When we finished, our appearances were disheveled. We tidied up, went back to our table, and drank some more. James paid our tab, then we left the restaurant. James drove me to my car parked at the Metro Station. We kissed and played around some more, then parted ways for the evening.

The next day, James came out of his office and told Judy he was going to the bank. In her usual facetious tone, Judy said, "Bring me back a couple thousand, okay." James looked back at me and smiled. When James returned to the office, he placed a bank envelope on my desk as he walked back to his office. In the envelope, there were twenty crisp one-hundred-dollar bills.

# CHAPTER FIVE

## REVERBERATIONS OF SAMENESS

"The unknowable is the beauty, the meaning the aspiration, the goal. Because of the unknowable, life means something. When everything is known, then everything is flat. You will be fed up."

~Osho

*Early the next morning, I had breakfast at a diner high up in the mountains of Rock Springs just above I-80W. Afterward, I gassed up my car and cautiously proceeded down a hill on which the diner was perched. Its elevation was so high that I gripped my steering wheel for fear I might lose control of my vehicle on the way down. That was scary! After waiting an interval at the STOP sign, I regained my composure, turned left onto I-80W, and continued my journey.*

*Gargantuan Tetons confronted me in the distance. That was humbling. The Rocky Mountains, the Tetons—everything in Wyoming is massive. In comparison, I felt like a small part of existence. The drive through Teton territory was tough, but I gained a greater appreciation for nature and creation.*

*Further along I-80W, I stopped at a gas station convenience store in Wyoming and bought some lottery tickets—Cowboy Draw, Mega Millions and Powerball. By late morning, it was sunny. I merged onto I-84W. When I saw the Welcome to Utah sign, I pulled over on the shoulder of the road and took a snapshot.*

*I got back into my car and continued driving the treacherous terrain, which was mostly at a high elevation. Whipsawed by my daily travels and the focus it required, I took a much-needed break from the road, exited the interstate, and pulled over at a 7-Eleven somewhere in Utah. Since crossing into Utah, I-84W had been accelerated predominantly by tight downhill curves, which gave it a racing effect. After driving for a while, I exited this road to refuel and reset the pace of my journey.*

* * *

I received a call from a law firm headquartered in Saint Louis about a bankruptcy legal secretary position in its Colorado office. At the end of the call, I booked a one-day, roundtrip flight to Denver.

As the plane made its descent for landing, I felt the rush of arriving in a new city. The plane landed in

Denver at 8:17 am. From Denver International Airport, the taxi driver merged onto the interstate and headed for downtown Denver. I observed the wide-open highway with the Rocky Mountains standing sovereignly in the backdrop. Along the way, I caught glimpses of street art on buildings amid the bustling crowds in the business district.

When the taxi arrived at Fifteenth and Wynkoop, I paid the driver and entered a sleek office building with bamboo-paneled walls and pristine marble floors. A large decorative raspberry-colored vase stood charmingly on a pedestal in the distance opposite the entrance. I entered the elevator, pressed a button and was ushered to a modern office with an elegant fishbowl encased in a wall.

I informed the receptionist of my interview, sat in a comfortable chair, and admired the firm's elegant interior. After a brief interval in the reception area, a woman appeared, greeted me and introduced herself as Edith Pomeroy, the firm's Office Administrator. A conservative-looking woman dressed in a collarless dark brown skirt suit simply adorned with a pearl necklace. Ms. Pomeroy escorted me to a small windowless conference room with a table and four chairs.

Two attorneys, Benjamin Benzwanger and Richard Halimaw, joined Ms. Pomeroy and me a short while later in the conference room. Following introductions and handshakes, Mr. Halimaw gave a brief overview of his practice. He made it clear that his current secretary's performance was less than satisfactory, which is why he was seeking a replacement.

As the interview progressed, general questions were asked of me, such as my level of experience with bankruptcy litigation, if I was comfortable handling difficult clients, and working under the pressure of tight deadlines. Finally, Mr. Halimaw wanted to know why I thought I was the best candidate for the position.

I gave a summary of my education, qualifications and experience. Petulant, Mr. Halimaw, a fast-talking uptight man, dismissed my response and shouted, *"What makes you different? I mean, sell yourself!"*

Ms. Pomeroy observed my unnerving surprise by Mr. Halimaw's abrasive comment and chimed in with a flimsy excuse in my defense. "Paige also has friends in Denver, and that is another reason she is looking to relocate."

Mr. Benzwanger continued with the interview explaining the details of his practice area as well as his requirements and expectations of his ideal assistant. At the end of the interview, Mr. Halimaw and Mr. Benzwanger left the interview in an awkward hurry. Ms. Pomeroy apologized to me for Mr. Halimaw's lack of discretion for a better word and told me that she would contact me with a decision when she was done interviewing the pool of candidates.

I left the interview feeling stunned and disappointed. I stood for a moment on the sidewalk outside the office building before walking to the corner of Sixteenth and Wynkoop and wondered if the lifestyle I imagined for myself in Denver was possible or even worth pursuing. I tried to escape the unpleasant recollection of my recent interview, but it stayed with me. So, I continued walking. I saw the words *Ice House* painted in large letters on the side of a red brick building. I stopped abruptly. I was standing in front of a building that had Becca's birthday on it: 817, the same time that my plane landed. At that moment, I recalled meeting Sharon on my connecting flight to Denver. During the flight, Sharon spoke with me at length about a psychic friend of hers that lives in Philadelphia. I remembered that I had the psychic's card Sharon had given me in my purse.

I made my own decisions, trusted my own judgment. But now, I was at a branch in the road. I felt conflicted. I was usually confident but felt less so now. I could not understand how the interview went awry. I knew that I disliked Mr. Halimaw's behavior and his harsh personality.

I sat down outside the Sixteenth Street bus station, reached inside my handbag for my cell phone, and dialed the psychic's number.

"Hello," the psychic answered.

"Hi, this is Paige. I was given your number by Sharon, a friend of yours, while on a flight to Denver today," I said.

"Paige, are you calling for a reading?" the psychic asked.

"Sort of," I said with a sigh. "I arrived in Denver today for an interview that didn't go very well. I'm not quite sure what to do."

"Well," the psychic continued, "I can certainly tell that you have a mind of your own."

I was taken aback by the psychic's comment, which offered no insight or resolution. The psychic continued, "Why don't you set an appointment with me. I'm available this Sunday at 10:00 am to discuss this with you further. That way, I can get a bead on you," the psychic added. "I accept VISA and Master-Card for private readings."

I set the appointment with the psychic and rang off. Afterward, I felt unsettled and angry—angry with myself for seeking the advice of a complete stranger about such a personal, life-altering decision. The psychic's comment provoked a rant within. *You won't get a bead on me or a read on me!* Right there, at the Sixteenth Street bus station in Denver, I decided that my decisions were mine to make. I knew that I would not keep my appointment with the psychic. To do so would mean surrendering my power of choice. I would not give that kind of power to anyone. For me, power was choice, and choice was freedom because the power of choice gave me the freedom to do as I pleased. I would not be held to deadlines or guidelines unless they were of my own making.

Gradually, I began to shape-shift into clarity. I saw clearly, felt better, became certain—certain that I wanted to live in a vibrant new city, that I could make a life for myself here, and that my visit to Denver was worthwhile.

But my optimism fluctuated as I remained somewhat ambivalent. After walking a few blocks, my confusion dissipated. An assortment of palatable aromas filled the mid-morning air. It kindled my appetite. I wandered into Qdoba, ordered my favorite edible taco bowl salad for an early *petit-dejeuner*, filled a cup with fountain soda, and took a table near a window to clear my thoughts and study the downtown scene.

From the restaurant window, I watched passersby while savoring forkfuls of my taco salad. I became absorbed in a reverie. I imagined what it would be like to live and work in Denver. Suddenly, I checked my watch. Realizing I had a surplus of time, I quickly wiped my mouth with a napkin, discarded the remnants of my meal, and left the restaurant.

Along Denver's touristy Sixteenth Street corridor, I browsed souvenir shops and admired the city's architecture. I found its seamless blend of historic and contemporary structures aesthetically appealing. By now, the sun had burned off the cool morning air. It turned into a surprisingly warm April day. I felt perspiration trickle down my back. I removed my blazer and carried it on my arm as I continued walking along, occasionally photographing landmarks with my cell phone. After several hours had passed, it was time for me to head to the airport.

Instead of darting back to DIA in a taxi, I purchased a bus ticket and took a more scenic route back to the airport. The time-conscious bus driver merged onto a highway and headed for the airport. I soaked in the scenery. As the bus approached DIA, the airport teepees came into view draped with the snow-capped Rocky Mountains in the distance. It was a thrilling feeling. There was a certain *je ne sais quoi* about Denver that embraced me. The Mile High air was fresh and crisp, people were radiant, physically fit and exuded a natural confidence. My emotions calmed. I wanted to be a part of the Denver community, its city and lifestyle. But I needed a job to afford it.

\* \* \*

It was a penitentiary of boredom.

A lull in the labor market lasted longer than expected. It was an economy pregnant with volatility. However, an economic upsurge brought with it a wave of new opportunities. That's how I landed at Gussie & Milsap, LLC, a small, but busy, law firm that specialized in the practice areas of insurance defense and bankruptcy.

Charleston, West Virginia, was a cultureless place. It reminded me of what I had read in history books about the depression era. Its buildings were old and dingy. When it rained, the gutters ran high and wreaked of garbage. Its overall mood was listless. Careless. Lifeless. Some of the city's real estate was so condemned and dilapidated, it was uninsurable, and much of its population was, sadly, obese.

Gussie & Milsap had its own brand of internal politics. It was a battleground and a contest. I witnessed verbal disputes among attorneys that spilled over into day-to-day staff relations affecting work performance and provoking disagreements among staff, making it difficult to focus. Overall, there was a lack of initiative that resulted in disorganized filing and inaccurate recordkeeping. I didn't know if this oversight was unintentional or deliberate. But after assessing the backlog of filing, I concluded that shirking the work had failed to develop a capacity to work.

I was told during my interview that there had already been five prior office administrators. So, I set an example, rolled up my sleeves and organized the heap of loose papers stacked on the copy room floor all the way up to the light switch on the wall. I brought order to the task by sorting the stack of papers into piles alphabetically on the conference room table.

In my role as Office Administrator, I also assisted Paul McCallick, the Managing Partner. At first, Paul assumed that I was familiar with filing litigation cases since I had worked for DC firms. But I told Paul that I knew very little about litigation procedures. So, Paul gave me a brief lecture on West Virginia's Rules of Civil Procedure.

On my own time, I read the state's rules, gained useful knowledge of litigation procedures, and before long, I was applying what I learned to daily tasks involving insurance defense and bankruptcy litigation. Within no time, I prepared Responses to Interrogatories, Requests for Admissions, and Requests for Production, and filed Quarterly Reports and Proof of Claims with local bankruptcy courts.

A typical day for me consisted of prparing for mediation, scheduling depositions, assigning court reporters to take depositions, which sometimes required a videographer. Paul frequently dictated cassette tapes for me to transcribe. He had a voice that resonated authority. However, I didn't take seriously his suggestion that we "hop right over there on the sofa" in his office. I ignored his invitation. Instead, I kept our work relationship professional and respectful.

You see, Paul's wife, Urma, also worked at Gussie & Milsap. She, too, was an attorney. In fact, Urma invited me to stay with them until I found a place of my own. During that time, we got to know each other quite well. They had toddler twins and a nanny who cared for them. Paul and Urma were very hospitable. Whenever they ordered out for dinner, they told me to get whatever I wanted, and they'd pay for it. They also let me stay rent-free in a beautiful, elaborately furnished bedroom—next to their bedroom. I also had my own private bathroom. When I returned home from work, my bathroom was always clean with fresh towels and washcloths. It was like staying at a five-star hotel. But after a few weeks, I could tell

Urma was getting skittish about me being at their house alone with her husband and their babies, while she worked late at the office. Next thing I knew, the alarm clock in my room started sounding off at odd hours in the early morning. I'm sure it was a wake-up call from Urma for me to get the hell out of their house.

After typing up initial drafts of mediation statements, I forwarded it to Paul for review. The exchange of draft documents was circulated from Paul to clients to Paul and back to me for revisions until the client and Paul agreed on a final draft. Once Paul signed off on legal documents, I scanned, emailed, faxed, and sent copies of the same via US Mail to all parties involved in the case.

Litigation was a fast-paced and interesting practice area. I was particularly meticulous about formatting documents, responding to client requests, and communicating with opposing counsel since Paul relied on me to handle these administrative aspects of his legal practice.

I was a do-it-yourselfer. I rarely delegated tasks because I didn't want to spend time explaining the details of assignments or waste time fixing someone else's mistakes. I wanted to know that the task was done right. If there were any mistakes, they would be my own, which I could easily find and fix. But lately, the volume of work grew increasingly intense, even for me. One of Paul's insurance clients made him primary counsel for all bad faith claims cases.

And, an insurance company had just hired Paul as their primary defense counsel. As a result, claims adjusters emailed at least five bad faith claims to our firm daily.

The increased workload led me to place an ad for an Office Assistant in the local newspaper. We needed someone to pick up and distribute mail, run bank errands, file documents with the court, pick up and deliver documents to the Office of the Secretary of State, organize legal correspondence, provide back-up reception relief, and update pleadings and discovery indices. I knew there would be a learning curve, but I also wanted to hire the right person for the job.

In the early stages of the interview process, I noticed one candidate's reluctance to shake my hand during introductions due to a difference in ethnicity. A second applicant dozed off to sleep during his interview then promptly awoke answering an unasked question, while a third candidate chose to wear a sundress to the interview showing off colorful tattoos. I wondered if any serious applicants would apply for the position. Then, I interviewed Freddie Jones.

Right away, I could see that Freddie was interested in the position and had the experience to do the job. Freddie had recently completed legal assistant training at a local community college. He was also looking for an entry-level position at a law firm. It was a perfect match! I offered Freddie the job, and he accepted.

After working at the firm for about a month, Freddie knew his assignments well. He took the initiative to set up conference rooms with refreshments in preparation for depositions, mediations and client consultations. One particular morning, Freddie entered a conference room to test the video cassette recorder for a deposition and to set up refreshments. But Freddie could not locate the VCR. In nervous haste, he approached me, asking about the VCR. We searched the office but couldn't find it. The deposition was less than two hours away. When Freddie told Paul that he couldn't locate the VCR for his deposition that morning, Paul sent out an email inquiring about the missing VCR. Conversations quickly escalated into accusations. Meanwhile, Trey, a partner, sent an email replying to all, stating that he had brought the VCR to the office as a courtesy, but since it was his VCR, he took it back home. To that, Paul replied that the VCR belonged to the office. Staff suddenly witnessed an email argument between Paul and Trey. In an accusatory tone, Trey emailed Paul, "Are you calling me a liar?" There was an explosion of chaos in the office, as employees sided with Paul or Trey.

The next morning when I arrived at work, Paul called me into his office. He told me that he was asked to leave the firm. Paul and Trey's recent email argument, in addition to other longstanding disagreements, forced the shareholders to choose sides. Paul told me that he was asked to leave because Trey's annual revenue exceeded his by three hundred thousand dollars. Paul assured me that his departure from the firm was for the best. He admitted to me that he hated Trey, and the two of them would never get along. Paul also told me that the firm had hired a new managing partner. Before Paul left the firm, he completed an evaluation of my performance that made me glow with pride.

While I was encouraged by Paul's evaluation of my performance as his assistant, in the coming months, I sensed something more than Paul's presence at the firm was missing.

I didn't exactly welcome the idea or reality of a new boss. Paul and I had a great work relationship, and we enjoyed working together. Now that Joseph Gerrard was the new managing partner, I expected the office dynamic to change. I just didn't know how.

I quickly learned that Joseph—a tall, pale-faced, pitchy-voiced man with blonde hair—was a micro-manager. Joseph preferred to dictate letters and pleadings for me to transcribe. Unlike Paul, Joseph didn't have the voice for it. Almost every evening after I left work, Joseph would dictate a letter which appeared electronically in my inbox via Winscribe. When I first began transcribing dictation for Joseph, I was annoyed by the decibel level of his dictation. Even with the volume turned all the way down, it sounded like he was dictating with a microphone.

One day, Freddie walked past my desk just as I put my foot on the pedal to start transcribing a letter that Joseph dictated. As I listened to the dictation through the headset, it began as all of Joseph's dictations had: "TYPE A LETTER!" Freddie backtracked and said, *"DAMN!* Why is he yelling on dictation tapes?"

*"Okay-kay-kay!"* I remarked jokingly, as we often did amongst ourselves when things at the office got too silly for an explanation. Then, I resumed transcribing the dictation.

After Paul left the firm, things got increasingly worse, especially since some of the staff envied my position.

Natasha, a paralegal, believed she was more deserving of and qualified for the Office Administrator position. She thought her tenure automatically qualified her for the job. But she wasn't considered. The Human Resources Manager, Doris, admitted that Natasha wanted the position for the wrong reasons. Natasha wanted the prestige of the position, but not the responsibilities that came along with it. From the outset, Natasha was uncooperative and resorted to manipulative tactics such as hiding office mail. This resulted in Urma, Paul's wife, defaulting on a hearing appearance that went un-calendared. Natasha worked tirelessly to sabotage my efforts as Office Administrator.

Rhonda, a legal secretary, who was also jockeying for the Office Administrator position, gave Urma an incomplete Witness and Exhibit List to take with her to a court hearing. During the hearing, Urma discovered that she didn't have a complete set of exhibits and called the office frantically demanding to speak with Rhonda about it. Rhonda sulked in the face of embarrassment, as it became clear that she had not provided Urma with the entire nine hundred-page document to take with her to court for the hearing.

Natasha and Rhonda constantly competed for my position. But their lack of attention to detail when handling their own workloads was compromised, which led Urma to contact Doris about their screw-ups.

Having worked a significant amount of overtime, I saved some money, which I used a portion of to finance the purchase of a new, fully-loaded 2.5 SL Nissan Altima—leather interior, heated seats, moon roof, and a head-turning sound system. I vacationed in Cancun for a week. The weekend following, I flew to Los Angeles. In time, I began to realize that my recent trips had been a sort of escapism from the small-town monotony. For instance, at the local grocery store, I noticed some customers pushing two carts—one with food and another with snacks such as potato chips, dips, ginger snaps, ice cream, doughnuts, candy bars, and cakes with thick icing. It was an inconvenient way of shopping that created longer checkout lines in an outmoded grocery store with no self-checkout lanes.

Standing in line was not one of my favorite things to do. Waiting exacerbated my patience, not to mention the extended exchange between customers and store clerks catching up on small town gossip. It was beyond boring. On one occasion, a customer and store clerk's discussion got so involved that the store clerk asked how the customer's pet rabbit was doing. *REALLY?!* I just wanted to pay for my groceries and get on to the next chore on my to-do list instead of listening to a bunch of country folk make a big deal about a damn bunny. But the chit-chat delayed my plans.

Compared to living in a big metropolitan city, West Virginia was unappealing. There were no fancy restaurants, upscale malls or contemporary residential communities. I longed to live in a big city brimming with things to do. There were not many, if any, African braiding salons in Charleston. So, I made a three-and-a-half-hour drive to Bignon's Braiding in Charlotte, North Carolina. Initially, I intended to drive to Charlotte the day after I returned from Denver, but instead, I relaxed two days, watched the NBA playoffs then drove to Charlotte.

Having endured eight hours of industrious braiding, I left the salon with eighteen-inch auburn micro-braids that complemented my complexion. Afterward, I was too tired to drive back to West Virginia that evening. So, I decided to stay the night in Charlotte. As I pulled into the parking lot of a hotel in downtown Charlotte, the oil light on my dashboard indicated mechanical maintenance was needed.

The next morning, while my car was being serviced, I walked to the heart of downtown Charlotte to feel the pulse of the city. I visited a museum, bought postcards and snapped pictures of landmarks. Charlotte is an artsy city. Before leaving, I had lunch at Qdoba.

I thought about lots of things while driving back home to West Virginia. After rethinking things: staff strife over my position, a temp's accidental ditching of ten bankruptcy binders, and all sorts of random or deliberate mishaps that occurred all too often, I contemplated—as I had since my visit to Denver—what life would be like for me there.

# CHAPTER SIX

## The High Life

"I've been hustling a nicely paid living out of
this life for a long time. . ."

~Anthony Bourdain, *Kitchen Confidential*

When I got back on the road, temperatures fluctuated
as I crossed state lines. I left behind a cool and breezy
Utah for an unexpected heatwave in Idaho. I drove a
moderate speed of sixty-five miles per hour, not due to
the heat, but because the next leg of my journey was
a distance of almost six-hundred miles. I encountered
road construction at various intervals along the way.
At one point, I was the lead car in a long line of vehicles that snaked along extended portions of I-84W under construction. The road construction had narrowed
down expansive interstate lanes to a two-way road of
traffic separated by seemingly endless miles of chan-
nelizer construction cones.

*After a while, I exited I-84W to take a respite from the road. I pulled up to a pump at a populated Shell gas station. A man perched high in a gleaming black, oversized four-by-four pick-up truck, with herculean tires that could conquer any terrain, pulled up to the gas pump beside me.*

*Frank introduced himself and offered to put gas in my car and pumped it, too. He told me that my Texas license plate caught his attention. He said he lived there years ago and struck up an immediate conversation. Frank invited me to join him for a late lunch at Burger King. I obliged.*

*Frank was pleasant and easy to talk to. He told me all about his life in the Air Force and his wife, whom he was picking up shortly before going to his second part-time job. We were having a delightful conversation. Then Frank asked, "Where are you headed?"*

*"Boise," I told him. I wasn't in the habit of telling strangers exactly where I was going.*

*"Do you have a place to stay?" he asked.*

*I thought it was awful nice of Frank to be concerned about me. However, I wasn't sure of his intentions. And, I was out here all alone on the road.*

*I told Frank, "I'll get a room at a hotel."*

*"Do you need money?" Frank asked.*

*My plan was to reach my destination safely, not get involved in a random hook-up.*

*"I appreciate your kind offer," I told Frank. "But I'll be fine, just the same."*

*When we finished eating, I thanked Frank for gassing up my car. Then, we went our separate ways.*

* * *

I threw caution to the wind. Irrepressible desires pulsating within wouldn't let me sleep through the night. One visit to Denver, and I was powerfully hooked.

I craved beauty, adventure, excitement. Denver was a mirror. I saw my reflection in this lively, lovely city! Everything about Denver beckoned good times ahead.

Upon further inspection, I discovered the distance to Colorado would be more than twenty hours—more than fifteen hundred miles. Was I ready for an adventure of a lifetime? For a good time, I will travel the distance. And, although what lay ahead appeared vague and unknown, its allure was magnetic. So I proceeded as planned.

On Memorial Day, I took to the road, beginning my trip on I-64 west. It was my first time driving in this direction. My senses were thirsty for the unknown. The road was open, and vehicles were sparse. I planned it that way, hoping my travels would be removed from traffic. I was challenging an inner fear of traveling on unfamiliar interstates in unknown directions.

I let my intuition guide me and enjoyed an eight-hour drive through Kentucky and Indiana to Mount Vernon, Illinois, where I stayed the night. Mount Vernon is a small town, where—believe it or not—horse and buggy traveled curbside along its roads. Preoccupied with driving, I was unable to capture a snapshot of this anachronism.

The next morning, I took to the road with the courage and stamina of a pioneer. Within no time, I found myself in St. Louis, Missouri—a happening place. While there, I stopped at Gibbol's, a novelty shop that sells clown and Halloween costumes, magic and juggling apparatus. I greeted the shop clerk, bought some postcards, then left and headed to Subway for lunch.

The weather was agreeable, so I sat at a table outdoors eating my tuna sub as I wrote notes on the postcards—my twenty-eight cent informants—to send to friends back home, letting them know I was on the road living *"The High Life."* I signed off on each postcard: *It's funBNme. Always living The High Life!* This became my postcard tagline. I pretty much branded myself with it.

A gust of wind suddenly blew my postcards off the table while my mind searched for a reason to hang out in St. Louis. The wind, however, was my indicator to get back on the road. I promised I would revisit St. Louis, but for now, I must get to Denver.

Traveling along I-70W, I conquered some of my interstate fears. I mean, what else could I do out here on major expressways in rush hour traffic? The further west I drove, the more engulfed I became in a sea of traffic. Soon, some of my inner fears abated and turned into excitement. *I was riding the wave of adventure!*

I've heard inspiring speeches and seen inspirational movies, but when I got passionate about *this adventure*, it fired up my dreams. I'm not sure if it was a lunar eclipse, but life had shaken things up and wouldn't let me live it in a mediocre way. Once empowered, I traveled fearlessly and hoped to inspire others—through my postcards—to do the same.

If you don't know, the Midwest can get blazingly hot. Now you know. When it became unbearable, I put up the windows, closed the moon-roof, and turned on the air conditioner. But most of all, I enjoyed driving with open windows, taking in the scent of fresh grass and fragrant flowers in full bloom.

*Ahhhhh.* Welcome to Kansas! This is the longest leg of my trip. I must drive through the entire state of Kansas!

The expanse of land driving along I-70W feels endless. Its distance is far and wide. I was awestruck! The beauty of nature in Kansas along I-70W certainly displays God's handiwork. Indeed, the land *is* good and plentiful. Livestock live well here!

WARNING: I gassed up my vehicle before venturing into Kansas and whenever my gas gauge reached half a tank. There are stretches of road along I-70W through Kansas, where no exits exist for miles. I didn't want to run out of gas anywhere out here on I-70W, especially not in Kansas. The land is too vast to traverse by foot and, traffic, at seventy-five miles per hour, is few and far between. Besides, I'd be a blur to drivers going ninety miles per hour in a seventy-five mile per hour zone.

Did I mention I had interstate fears? They're gone! With wildlife running rampant, I became exceedingly perspicacious while driving along I-70W. If anyone can travel the distance of Kansas in a day, God bless them. I was not doing nonsense! I drove six hours for the day, exited I-70W at Topeka, Kansas, a thriving, contemporary city, bought my favorite taco bowl at Qdoba, and checked in to a nearby Sleep Inn for the evening.

By 6:40 am, I was in my car. The weather started out pleasantly enough—low 60s. Gradually, the sun rose and stood above Kansas, radiating its powerful summer heat. Herds of livestock—tails dancing in the wind—grazed happily in grassy meadows.

Kansas is a complex mix of intense heat with high, gusty winds. The wind was so powerful; its impact visibly swayed eighteen-wheelers. *Now that's powerful!* So, I didn't try to bypass or overtake any of these oversized trucks on a curve. *It's dangerous!*

Driving through the Midwest for the first time, I felt I was creating my own adventure. I knew Colorado was mountainous but had no idea if I would find myself driving on narrow, twisty mountain roads without barriers. But I was up for the challenge— driven by the excitement of the unknown. The risk-taker within had coaxed me way out West, and there was no turning back. Like birth, I had reached a point where my only direction was forward.

Out here like a bird on a wire, enjoying my delicious freedom, like VISA, everywhere I want to be, having an ineffable experience! Now, whenever I feel a desire to break free, I never miss an opportunity to experience expansion. Imagination *is* powerful, but nothing ever becomes real until it is experienced.

I'd like to interject something here. Desires are meant to be experienced, and dreams are meant to be fulfilled. But, when full potential and self-expression are suppressed, repressed and suffocated, it morphs into tortuous yearnings that solidify into regrets—unfulfilled passions that procrastination continuously prevents—creating endless inner torment.

I fear regret more than the unknown. And, more than anything, I fear the feeling of regret, which sparked this adventure. I plan to experience all the joy I can! I don't want dreams to die inside of me unlived. My Inner Spirit applauded me for taking this journey, allowing it to actively participate instead of just observe.

Driving the distance of I-70W, I let my experience unfold on its own, relishing the now. I realized that first time experiences are once-in-a-lifetime occurrences because they can never be experienced again for the first time. I savored this moment, without really keeping track of where I am on my journey (signs and time will do that); I relaxed and enjoyed this moment in time.

Kansas kept me guessing. What's over that hill? Around that bend? Down that meadow? But the size of wildlife and roadkill also kept me car-bound. Besides, I was so close to Denver, my hands were practically glued to the steering wheel. Occasionally, I encountered stretches of road bloody with hoofs, innards and other remnants of wildlife unsuccessful at crossing I-70W.

Welcome to Colorado!

With Denver in close proximity, a surge of thrilling sensations flooded through me. I reveled in delight and stopped to gas up my car. When the interstate lanes expanded, I knew I was on the outer limits of a major city. In Denver, I-70W expanded to eight lanes.

On June 1, five o'clock rush hour traffic welcomed me to Denver. *The Mile High City!*

It took a while, but when traffic permitted, I exited I-70W at 38th and Park Avenue and made my way to downtown Denver. As I rounded Blake Street, I was immediately introduced to the very prominent Coors Field, surrounded by opulent residential and commercial real estate, local cafés, and popular restaurants. *The Cheesecake Factory!*

The pulse and beauty of downtown Denver is like a flawless diamond—stunningly engaging.

As dusk emerged, it brought with it a low-hanging moon that appeared approachably brighter. I checked into the Quality Inn Central, a high-rise hotel with spectacular mountain views. I showered, dressed and went to the restaurant downstairs. I sat at the bar and ordered a glass of Merlot to unwind while

I watched a playoff game and waited for my steak dinner. After two glasses of wine and a savory meal, I felt exhaustion setting in. I experienced a stimulus overload. So, I paid my tab and went to my room, where I nodded in and out of sleep before finally retiring for the evening.

Awakened by the warmth of the summer sun, I dressed and proceeded to live *The High Life*.

\* \* \*

Later that afternoon, I drove to downtown Denver to meet with Tara McNamara, a recruiter at an employment agency, about a paralegal position at a law firm in Colorado Springs.

After registering with the agency and completing a skills assessment exam, Tara scheduled an interview for me to meet with the office administrator at 2:00 pm the next day in Colorado Springs. As our meeting ended, Tara walked with me to the elevator to give some last-minute interview tips.

So far, I was pleased with my long-distance endeavor. I took the elevator downstairs and exited the building. I felt a sense of fulfillment. It was nearing the close of business as I walked a short distance to a lot where my car was parked. I paid the attendant and merged into traffic, taking Broadway to I-25 South toward Colorado Springs.

Lots of drivers were going in the same direction, resulting in gridlock. I was trapped for a time in bumper to bumper traffic with trucks transporting crane and rigging tractors, diesel fuel, and time-sensitive cargo such as dairy, produce and overnight mail. Sitting in my car in this unfamiliar city, I felt intimidated by the intensity of commercial transport traveling on the interstate during rush hour. But after some reflection, I recalled my entire journey to Denver had been a constant flux of wide load cargo being transported to and fro. This was the Midwest. Things were different. People were different. There was vast, unchartered territory to explore, such as Garden of the Gods, Estes Park and Pikes Peak. Adventure summoned.

As traffic progressed, I-25 became a racetrack. I mounted a steep curve that suddenly sloped. As I glanced in my rearview mirror, an oversized truck approached my vehicle at top speed. The truck driver sharply changed lanes forcing me to grip my steering wheel to avoid a tailspin as the impact of the wind-speed from this hurtling diesel tanker sped by, shaking my car. Then, a motorcyclist without a helmet vroomed by as the high-powered popping of his motor faded in the distance. Nestled in the leather interior of my Altima, I settled in for the long drive.

Beyond Castle Rock, the road narrowed to two lanes, and the setting shifted into a backdrop of scenic high country. Rolling hills cloaked I-25 with alluring vistas hugging ravine-like curves constructed with a prescience to preserve nature. Ineffable splendor was everywhere. Yet, an attempt to describe the detail of its grandeur would only discredit its panorama. So, I marveled at it and allowed my senses to luxuriate in its impressiveness.

Entering the city limits, I saw "Welcome to Colorado Springs" chiseled on a huge stone, while a banner wiggling in the wind welcomed visitors to a Women's Golf Tournament. I could see the Quality Suites sign, where I planned to stay, towering in the distance.

After settling in, I drove to a nearby diner for dinner, returned to my room and unpacked some of my belongings. Exhausted, I lingered in a hot shower. Refreshed and relieved to finally be in Colorado Springs, I lounged on the hotel bed while watching the NBA Playoffs. My mood was reminiscent of recent days spent driving way out west to parts unknown. As I reflected on my journey through a curtainless window, Venetian blinds cast slivers of sun rays into fading shadows on the hotel wall. I dozed off to sleep.

I arrived five minutes early for my interview with the Colorado Springs law firm. I met with Connie Duvall, the office administrator. After a brief meeting with her, Ms. Duvall introduced me to Alex Kennedy, an attorney. Mr. Kennedy proceeded to interview me for the position. He greeted me and explained the scope of his practice. He also outlined qualities that he looked for in an assistant. Then, Mr. Kennedy asked me why I moved to Colorado. When I told Mr. Kennedy that I moved to Colorado all by myself, his expression turned to concern. The interview took on a serious tone, which suddenly became an interrogation. Mr. Kennedy judged me.

In his eyes, I was a pleasure-seeking gad-about. He assumed I was a run-around, not the settle-down type. While Mr. Kennedy told me that my adventure to Colorado was courageous, the furrow in his brow also told me that he found it alarming. Mr. Kennedy concluded the interview. We shook hands, and I left him with his discordant feelings as I proceeded down the hall with Ms. Duvall. I also thanked Ms. Duvall for her time. We shook hands, and I left the office. I didn't expect a follow-up call and didn't receive one.

I felt that a part of my world had been reconfigured as a result of moving to Denver, not only because I was in a different time zone, but because Denver somehow represented a shift from the norm. I had taken a risky leap of faith that put me on an adventurous new path of possibilities. Now, more than ever, I lived in the moment, which demanded my immediate adjustment. My new environment challenged me to break with old patterns of familiarity that once defined my security. As I did, life sort of became an experiment.

I registered with a local Workforce Center and went on an intensive job search, emailing and faxing my resume to law firms. Two weeks later, I received a voicemail from Lucy Fulkner, a law firm recruiter in Denver. When I returned her call, Lucy introduced herself and discussed the position in more detail. She wanted to interview me for a bankruptcy paralegal position at Ludlow & Bulani, LLP in Denver.

The next day, I drove seventy miles to Denver for an interview with Lucy that lasted ten minutes. Still in the stratosphere from my recent travels to Denver, I was caught off guard after exiting the elevator. It faced a heavy metal door with a small square glass in the center of it. I pressed an intercom button on the wall that allowed me to communicate with the receptionist inside the office. Once I was identified, the bolt was unlocked. What type of firm is this, I thought? It was the first time I encountered a firm with such heightened security. Usually, reception areas were open and inviting. Ludlow & Bulani, on the other hand, gave me the impression that its employees were closely monitored and had little freedom.

Once inside, I re-introduced myself to the receptionist. After a brief interval, Lucy walked up to me and introduced herself. We took a flight of spiraling internal stairs to Lucy's office.

Lucy complimented my résumé and told me she was impressed with my bankruptcy and litigation experience. Then, with exuberant enthusiasm, Lucy asked with beaming interest about my travels to Denver. She wanted to know all about it and invited me out for happy hour with a group of her girlfriends to talk about it in detail. Lucy welcomed me to Denver, recommended landmark sights to see, and before I knew it, my interview with Lucy was over. Lucy told me that she would invite me back to meet with the attorneys.

The following day, I drove seventy miles back to Denver for an interview with attorneys at Ludlow & Bulani that lasted maybe ten minutes. After a very brief interview, I decided to take a day trip to Cheyenne, Wyoming. It was only one hundred miles or so away. I could drive that in an hour, I thought.

Once I bypassed Boulder, I felt out of my element. I got way out there, and the terrain of the road got the better of me. But I pushed on. It was a scenic drive. I saw Terry's Bison Ranch along the way and drove by a landmark doing eighty miles per hour. I made a U-turn in state trooper territory and looped around to take a snapshot of the "Welcome to Wyoming" sign. After doing so, as I walked back to my car, an eighteen-wheeler flew by. The impact of its wind speed nearly knocked me to the ground. I stumbled back, gathered myself, and approached my car again—this time with caution. It was another lesson I learned about the "rules of the road" during one of my high life adventures.

I pulled into Love's Travel, a roadside gas station convenience store to get some refreshments and postcards. While sitting at a table writing notes on postcards and sipping cranberry grape juice, my eyelids started getting heavy with fatigue. But this was not the time for a nap. I still had to drive one hundred and seventy miles back to Colorado Springs. After placing stamps on my postcards, I took the twenty-eight-cent informants to the Diesel Desk, which served as an official mailbox out here in the rural West.

A week or so later on July 4, Lucy called me. She apologized for calling me on a holiday but told me that the attorneys had made a decision and wanted me to start as soon as possible. Lucy was throwing an elaborate Fourth of July party—fireworks and all. She invited me to her home for the festivities.

# CHAPTER SEVEN

## Don't Crack Under Pressure

> "If an unexpected period of unemployment inspires you to leap off a bridge, hang yourself from a tree or chug-a-lug a quart of drain cleaner, that's too bad."
>
> ~Anthony Bourdain, *Kitchen Confidential*

*I merged onto I-84W. This part of my journey became increasingly grueling because it turned into an uphill, winding climb that just wouldn't let up. I was concerned about pulling hills because the only cargo I brought along with me aside from my clothes, shoes and small personal belongings was a wooden, two-drawer desk. Since the drawers couldn't be removed from the desk, its weight became a concern as my ascent along I-84W continued. I hoped the desk remained secured in the trunk of my car.*

*When the road expanded again, some impatient drivers accelerated above the speed limit. One of them cut me off to make the next exit. But I wasn't about to waste time or energy on a nameless, faceless driver, so didn't even give him the finger.*

*I started off kicking asphalt, but after driving hundreds of miles, my journey had worn me down. I was tired—physically and mentally. My focus was lapsing from overexertion and exhaustion. I pulled off the road in Meridian, Idaho to get something to eat and to recharge.*

*I stopped in a shopping center at a Subway sandwich shop. I bought a tuna sub, Coca Cola, and a chocolate chip cookie. I got back in my car to eat my sandwich and to drive as far as daylight hours would allow. Much later, I woke up to a flashlight shining on my face from outside my car window.*

*It was a police officer. By now, it was dark outside. In the middle of eating my meal and making plans to continue driving, I had fallen asleep. I put the window down half-way, and the officer asked for my driver's license and registration. I gave it to him and told him about my journey to the Pacific Northwest. After the officer cleared me, he recommended a nearby hotel.*

\* \* \*

In my new position as Bankruptcy Paralegal in Denver, my tasks involved a barrage of administrative tasks as well as billable responsibilities that included reviewing Chapter Eleven Plans and e-filing petitions with bankruptcy courts. Although I had acquired bankruptcy and litigation experience while working at Gussie & Milsap in West Virginia, the attorneys at Ludlow & Bulani, LLP insisted that I attend official training to get acclimated to Colorado's Rules of Civil Procedure. So, the firm paid for my bankruptcy and litigation training courses with the bankruptcy and local courts.

When I returned to the office, I noticed some of my co-workers appeared dazed from spending too much time staring at their computers. I was careful to organize my work so that I avoided focusing on my computer screen for extended periods of time. I switched off to different tasks such as opening and scanning mail or returning calls to clients.

In addition to handling bankruptcy matters, I was also responsible for receiving, reviewing and accepting new referrals from clients for HOA delinquent assessments. It was an assignment that involved searching county assessor's websites to determine record owners of properties. After determining the ownership status of a property, it was my responsibility to contact the homeowners associations to request updated ledgers that reflected current amounts due for delinquent assessments. Then, after assessment arrears had been accurately computed, I drafted demand letters to borrowers and lenders informing them of their obligation to pay delinquent assessments. When borrowers called in response to the demand letters, it was my job to inform them of their delinquent assessments and remind them of their obligation to pay.

The litigation aspect of notifying borrowers to collect delinquent assessments involved sending Orders Regarding Stipulations between plaintiffs and defendants, including payoff checks to HOA counsel for payment of unpaid assessments. I also obtained recorded copies of Transcripts of Judgments from county clerk and recorder's offices. As if I didn't already have enough of my own work to do, I assisted Laura, another paralegal, with mailing out a Motion for Summary Judgment to eighteen parties on the Certificate of Service.

When Anne Marie, a paralegal that assisted attorneys with litigation matters and deficiency actions, heard about me assisting Laura, she began telling her attorneys that she was overwhelmed with her workload. She liked to reminisce aloud about the "good ol' days" at Ludlow & Bulani, when the office had more of a family feel to it. But, according to Anne Marie, that was more than a decade ago. Since that time, the firm had grown and increased in size with offices in Wyoming and Nevada. Anne Marie, now married with a family of her own, appeared stuck in how things used to be instead of growing with the changing times.

Anne Marie's husband, Curtis, also worked at the firm, but in a different department downstairs. She was always going down there, checking up on him.

What worried Anne Marie most were the attractive women now working at the firm. I was one of them, and Anne Marie had her suspicions. She looked at me with concern, the way that married women do when they feel threatened by another woman's beauty.

One day, Heidi, one of Anne Marie's attorneys, asked if I could help out with Anne Marie's workload. According to Heidi, Anne Marie needed to leave early afternoons to pick up her son from daycare until she could find a new babysitter. Now, in addition to my own assignments, I was saddled with Anne Marie's workload for however long. In the days following Heidi's request, I observed Anne Marie doing little to no work and spending most of her time lollygagging with other paralegals. I could see in the faces of many of my co-workers that the daily grind had nearly pulled some of them under the wheel. We all left each day assured that the work would be there waiting for us when we returned.

I now no longer had to make a one-hundred-forty mile commute to work in Denver from Colorado Springs and back. Moving to Denver shaved one-hundred twenty-eight miles off my daily commute. What a relief! Later that afternoon, after unpacking and organizing my new kitchen, I took a break and went to H-Mart to buy groceries. I also bought a bottle of wine to celebrate my accomplishment.

After attending bankruptcy and litigation training courses at the courts, I felt better equipped to do my job. When I returned to the office, there were numerous ECF notifications in my inbox. I sifted through my emails, which included reminders of pending assignments from attorneys as well as paralegals. Since there were no legal secretaries at this firm, paralegals functioned in both capacities.

In the weeks that followed, I spent the majority of my time on PACER, familiarizing myself with assigned Chapter Eleven cases and documenting the most recent activity on an Excel spreadsheet. My Chapter Eleven caseload consisted of more than one hundred bankruptcy cases in multiple jurisdictions, some of which involved property appraisals.

In the coming months, I saw waves of daily emails from Emily, the firm's human resources manager. Emily's emails provided staff with a list of employees that no longer worked at the firm. The ration of caseload to employee was staggering. Yet, staff whose performance buckled under the pressure of the grind were shown the door or left the firm without giving proper notice. Although replacements were quickly hired, some new hires often led to similar outcomes—*turnover was high.*

Whenever employees left the firm of their own volition or were terminated, Emily indicated in her emails a change in the office's security access code. Gradually, Emily's emails stopped altogether. I suppose the ongoing announcement of staff departures was lowering employee morale. To boost it, one of the bankruptcy attorneys bought lunch from Chipotle for the entire bankruptcy staff. *It worked.*

Some of the bankruptcy staff looked forward to coming to work, if only for the free lunch. They doubled-down, worked hard and took ownership of their work—at least for a while. Still, some staff were quitting under the radar. It just wasn't broadcast in the usual way. Now, Emily's emails only communicated a change in the office's security access code. But there continued to be a constant rotation of new faces.

I considered the irony of working here: the volume of caseload drove the business, yet the workload promoted an environment of escapism. I felt I was working double-time to keep up with corralling bankruptcy files in preparation for hearings, contacting court clerks to obtain trial dates and hearing dates, not to mention attending weekly meetings to provide status updates on HOA delinquent assessments and foreclosure litigation cases. The latter was a bore. From week to week, there were no significant changes to report in the foreclosure litigation cases.

Irene, or Reenie, as she preferred to be called, had been working at Ludlow & Bulani for the past twenty-six years. I was told that someone besides Reenie needed to know the history of litigation cases since Reenie was nearing retirement. The attorneys' main concern was that the work continued.

As work seemed to be everyone's priority, I noticed attendance was, too. A few weeks later, Jenna, a paralegal that occupied a workstation next to me, told me that she wanted to take a vacation, but she dreaded returning to a massive amount of emails in her inbox. The thought of work and emails piling up during her absence worried Jenna. Employee's workloads had become so overwhelming that it made some staff consider taking a vacation, but many decided against it. However, Emily urged employees to take time off for vacations to avoid physical burnouts or meltdowns.

One day, while searching for the firm's office locations on the Internet, I came across an article about Ludlow & Bulani, LLP that revealed the firm was under investigation for fraudulent billing and sketchy business practices. The article stated that "Lawyers at the firm charged nearly six times the market rate for posting legal notices on a homeowner's property." According to the article, a series of investigations revealed that the firm had engaged in foreclosure fraud.

I was shocked, especially since there had been no discussion of an investigation at the office. I wondered if other employees knew about the investigation but were pretending to go about business as usual. I didn't share my findings with anyone else at the firm, but I did observe and listen more closely.

Not knowing what to expect next, given the ongoing investigation into Ludlow & Bulani's involvement in foreclosure fraud, I was on tenterhooks—to put it mildly. I took day trips most weekends to explore the Midwest and to relieve some of the tension I had about the firm's future and my place in it. I got adventurous one holiday weekend and drove to Des Moines, Iowa.

I found driving long distances throughout the Midwest rather therapeutic. It was a time of renewal and healing from grief. I lost my mother nearly a year ago. Observing nature—trees, mountains, wildlife—helped to put things into perspective for me. I became self-attuned and introverted. I pondered the meaning of life, thought about my accomplishments and failures, and considered my long-term goals. It was a time of solitude. I pruned from it the realization that I'd become one of the topmost branches in my family tree.

Traveling along I-76 east, a heavy odor of cattle piss and dung hung in the air for miles. Interstate 76 can take you many places, namely, Scottsbluff, Council Bluffs and Des Moines. When driven its extent, I-76 east converts to I-80 east, a never-ending road to almost anywhere—Chicago, Kansas City and beyond. But when driven at night, I-76 west turned into a virtual blind man's bluff with its sudden dips in the road, sharp curves and roaming wildlife. Since my driving skills didn't rival Danica Patrick's, I followed an eighteen-wheeler at least two car lengths distance. Having decided at dusk *not* to check into a hotel, here I was out on I-76 at night—with just my eyesight and headlights—playing "High Plains Drifter" in the formidable darkness of a starless sky. I recalled the line from a classic movie: *Darkness is the restful gift of God.* So, I relaxed in the comfort and security of my fully-loaded Nissan Altima and made my way safely back to Denver. At the end of my journey, I took a hot shower then went to bed.

The second time I drove to Iowa, I noticed a sign posted along I-76E warning drivers against picking up hitchhikers because a prison was in close proximity. I found myself in a peculiar situation when a woman begged me to take her to her home-town—Des Moines.

We had a brief conversation about the sweltering summer heat at 104 degrees when I casually mentioned to this woman that I had approximately one hundred and twenty-three miles to go before I reached Des Moines. She pleaded with me to take her with me. She said she had been stranded at this gas station convenience store for the past four days without food, and that the store clerks were kind enough to give her water and let her come inside the store out of the heat. She even volunteered her ID showing it to me. I noticed her middle name was the same as Becca's and one of my aunt's first name. I agreed to take the woman along with me to Des Moines. When she got inside my car, she said, "I can't tell you how good this seat feels against my back." Then, she fell asleep.

On another occasion, I drove five-hundred and sixty-two miles to Missouri. When I got back home, I was so tired, I was certain I was done road-tripping, but the magnetism of adventure had me back on the road sooner than I thought. Days later, I was headed for my next adventure, New Mexico! The Land of Enchantment.

I entered New Mexico via I-25S and encountered gorgeous mountainous vistas with dizzying precipices. Along the way, I saw signs cautioning "Gusty Winds Likely" and "Curves Tighten." But nowhere was there any indication to drivers that the roads slope so steep, vehicles tilt at intense angles. I'm terribly afraid of heights.

Gibraltar-like mountains with heavy quarry resting at its foothills stood authoritatively like monuments along this interstate, adorned with fabric similar to the texture of a woman's stocking to protect against falling rock. "*Aaaaah*," I thought humorously, "I feel so secure." On the way home from Ratan, I found myself enraptured by another summer sunset as dusk quickly covered the sky. These were the tales of my road trip adventures I emailed to friends with photos entitled "Pictures That Tell a Story."

While my adventures were therapeutic, they became a form of escapism from the imminent future of Ludlow & Bulani, and a deeper underlying issue—a longstanding unresolved issue I had with my eldest sister, Harriet. She didn't attend our mother's funeral. I had a HUGE problem with that. Not only did Harriet not attend our mother's funeral, she completely obliterated our mother's name from her vocabulary. Yet, Harriet expected us to have an agreeable sibling friendship in the face of it.

Like a pus-filled sore, my sibling relationship with Harriet festered and couldn't heal. I made a big move from Colorado to Texas to resolve our differences. But after six weeks of Harriet's nagging, threats and accusations, I left her place and made my own way in Texas. I was better for it. Over the next four months, I won fourteen thousand five hundred dollars playing the Daily Four lottery.

Now, I understood why my mother had become so bitter about a decade before she died. She felt all the nurturing, time and care that she had given us had gone unrecognized, unappreciated, and that it wasn't good enough. But I told my mother, on her sickbed at a nursing home a year before her passing, that she raised us right and gave us the best life she could, considering that our fathers weren't really there for us. I made sure our mother didn't take on the mental burden of feeling like a failure for decisions we made in our own lives. "We all grew up in the same household with the same set of rules," I said. Favoritism aside, we all got our asses whupped if we didn't obey or do our chores. I made the choice to obey my mother, and things worked out fine between us.

At the beginning of 2014, the bad blood that Monica instigated blew up in my face in the form of an email. It was sent to me under the guise of my nephew's name and contained such an overwhelming amount of profanity it was blasphemous. While I wasn't sure who sent the email, it was clear that someone in my own family obviously disliked me.

So, I pivoted out of their lives and left them to sort out their own discordant feelings.

Along the way, state to state and shortly after relocating to the Pacific Northwest, I mailed a postcard to Monica, letting her know that I had relocated. The news of my move to the Pacific Northwest spread like wildfire. The next thing I knew, Harriet contacted me via email. She asked, "How difficult was it to drive to the Pacific Northwest?" I replied to her email providing a brief account of my travels.

A week or so later, I received another email from Harriet saying she had participated in a Skype interview for a job in the Pacific Northwest. She added that she'd read an article in *U.S. News & World Report* on the city's economy. All of a sudden, Harriet was doing everything she could to re-situate herself in the Pacific Northwest. Go figure! But I've always held the belief that people will self-correct when left to their own devices.

Monica sprung a surprise on me when she told me that Harriet was planning a trip to visit me in the Pacific Northwest. Mind you, I knew nothing about it. Harriet had not so much as mentioned a word to me about her plans. As far as I knew, Harriet was about to start a new job in Florida and moved to an apartment closer to her new job. I couldn't trust either of them. These were some tricky bitches, which is why Richard warned me: "Deal with them with a long-handled spoon." And, beat them over the head with it if you have to.

My Great Aunt Vivienne played similar games. She was my grandmother Katie's sister. By now, Aunt Vivienne had to be almost ninety years old, but she was messy in her heyday.

I remember Harriet telling me that she purchased an Amtrak ticket to visit Aunt Vivienne. Then, unexpectedly, Aunt Vivienne told her that her back was bothering her, and she didn't want any company. This left Harriet holding the ticket and having to eat the loss of the cost. At the time, Harriet and I were twenty-somethings. I laughed myself into a belly-ache over Aunt Vivienne's deception.

Some years later, when I moved to West Virginia, I sent Aunt Vivienne a postcard letting her know I'd relocated. She invited me to New York for Christmas. Since this would be my first Christmas in West Virginia, I didn't feel up to traveling to New York. So, I sent Aunt Vivienne a holiday card telling her I decided to spend Christmas at home in my new apartment. But the last time I had spoken with Aunt Vivienne, she urged me to get my airline ticket because she was looking forward to seeing me.

A few days later, I arrived home from work to a message on my answering machine. It was Aunt Vivienne canceling our holiday plans. More than a decade later, Aunt Vivienne gave the same excuse. She said she was having back pains and didn't want to play hostess during the holiday. Aunt Vivienne often let the bottom fall out of her promises. But it didn't matter. I side-stepped her deception. I didn't bother to return her call. My holiday card was my informant. After receiving it, Aunt Vivienne didn't speak to me again until some years later.

Recently, Harriet texted me Aunt Vivienne's cell phone number. However, I was reluctant to call Aunt Vivienne because she had a tendency to try to one-up me. She did that when I told her I relocated to Denver. Aunt Vivienne loved to steal the spotlight. But this time, I intended to savor my own success. I took Richard's advice.

# CHAPTER EIGHT

## LIVING IN SUSPENSE

*"When you've been keeping secrets long enough, you can sense when other people are doing the same."*

*~Pearson* (TV series)

*The next morning before leaving Meridian, I bought a breakfast sandwich and chocolate milk. I was on the road pre-dawn to get a head start on the morning traffic. I kept driving until I reached Ogden and crossed into Oregon. From the direction I approached it, Oregon was out in the middle of nowhere. The road consisted of loose, gravelly rocks, the kind that tend to get lodged in tire treads. I continued driving, mounting a high hill. When I reached the top, it revealed a picturesque mountainous terrain. I spent the next hundred miles or so driving through severe curves and punishing peaks high up in the mountains. There was no let-*

*up for a long, long time and no shoulder to pull over on. My only direction was forward, so I pressed on. I passed by the Oregon Trail.*

\* \* \*

I almost got sick on the Dart train on the way home from work one evening. After eight months of living in Dallas, I was still homesick for Denver. I couldn't seem to make the adjustment. I yearned for Denver like a forlorn lover. No more Rocky Mountains. No day trips to Estes Park or Garden of the Gods. I was edgy, angst and angry. Although I missed Denver terribly, now was not the time to reconsider. I'd just received a call from a recruiter about a temp-to-perm position in downtown Dallas. Before I accepted, I asked the recruiter where the office was located. I didn't want to work anywhere near West End.

In case you don't know, West End is skid row for derelicts. It's in the heart of downtown Dallas. All manner of illicit activity goes on there. It's a hub of visibly neglected people against the backdrop of a working population. When I first took Dart public transit to downtown Dallas for an interview, I was horrified as the train pulled up to this dirty station. I hadn't witnessed the likes of such mindless roaming, underhanded exchange, and lazy languishing since my childhood days in Valley Green. I couldn't believe such shenanigans were going on in Dallas's downtown business district. So, before de-boarding the train, I asked another passenger, "Is this downtown Dallas?"

"Yes," the passenger responded assuredly.

When the doors opened, I stepped off the train and found myself thrust into a flurry of wanton activity. I kept my eyes focused on where I was going as I made my way through crops of crowds planted on the sidewalk. Back in DC, my friend Becca and I coined a phrase: "Class recognize class." Suddenly, I felt like an heir of Jesus Christ as a sea of people parted to let me through. Then, a swell of them followed me with burgeoning questions and offers.

"Can you spare some change?"

"Hey, you tryin' to buy some batteries? Soap?"

"I got those phone chargers."

I swear for God, I thought. If one of these mutha-fuckas touch the hem of my garment—

I tended to attract some jokers in the deck.

Harold Gykeman wanted to arm-twist the world into submission. For instance, whenever his wife, Evelyn, called the office, she had little say-so in family matters. Since Harold was the breadwinner, he made all the family decisions. Like the time Harold appointed his sister, Anna, to pick up his daughter, Jessica, from the airport the day before Thanksgiving. Despite Jessica's pleas for her brother, Daniel, to meet her at the airport, Harold was adamant in his decision. He dismissed Jessica's appeals and insisted that Aunt Anna pick her up. Jessica had been away at college and just wanted to spend a little time with her big brother since they had seen very little of each other. But by the end of their call, Jessica was unhappy. Harold, on the other hand, emerged from his office with his nose at an upward angle. He displayed an air of victory. After all, he was a lawyer consumed with winning arguments.

Harold, a partner attorney, intimidated some of the staff at Bossett, Giles & Langford, P.C. Associate attorneys spoke highly of him, as did support staff, but more-so from a place of fear than respect. Harold undermined his colleagues and criticized them when their work product didn't measure up to his standards. Harold was quick to report staff to management if he felt they were unresponsive to his concerns. And, employees who didn't cooperate with his demands were reprimanded, written-up or worse—*fired*.

Harold needed others to cater to his ego. Whenever he felt anyone was less than forthcoming or remiss, he obnoxiously exclaimed, *"Excuse me!"* A familiar phrase I knew all too well. It was a statement that prefaced a disagreement of sorts when Harold felt misunderstood.

I was Harold's third secretary in the past two years. His first secretary, Olivia, left the firm during her lunch hour and never returned. Harold had sneezed on her while dictating a letter over her shoulder as she typed. He didn't bother to apologize or excuse himself.

His next secretary, Faustine, felt pressured by

his constant questioning. His presumptuous inquiries into her personal affairs made Faustine uncomfortable. However, she was reluctant to say so. Faustine feared doing so would jeopardize her employment with the firm. Skittish after only eight months of working at the firm, Faustine told Harold that she was relocating to Kansas City to be near her sister and niece—family that no one had ever heard Faustine speak of before. Although many of her co-workers suspected that she lied about moving out of town, they were somewhat certain that Faustine's temporary tenure was due to Harold's prying. In the days leading up to her departure, Faustine looked agitated, and her conversation with staff was terse. Whatever bothered Faustine gnawed at her internally like arsenic. But Faustine remained silent, opting to leave the firm rather than risk a verbal confrontation or trying to resolve her real concerns with Harold.

Unwilling to accept that he was to blame for yet another secretary's departure from the firm, Harold quickly dismissed any reservations about Faustine's decision to leave the firm and proceeded to contact Priyal, the Office Administrator, to arrange interviews for a replacement.

When Faustine left, Jill Langford, a name partner, who shared an assistant with Harold, requested a new secretary. Without a secretary, Jill's workload suffered tremendously, and administrative tasks were piling up. There were unreconciled expense reimbursements, cassette tapes that needed transcribing, an overflow of attorney time entry to bill, and a back-log of filing to organize. Grant Bossett, the managing partner at Bossett, Giles & Langford, honored Jill's request for a new secretary and paired Jill with the secretary in his group. Jill was thrilled to finally be out of Harold's group. She knew that Harold was re-sponsible for the high turnover of secretaries within their group, but the backlash of Harold's anger kept Jill from confronting him to discuss it. Eventually, Harold decided on a new temporary replacement secretary.

During a conversation in the office cafeteria, I overheard Harold ask Jill why she changed attorney groups. Jill told Harold that his group consisting of five attorneys generated too much work for one sec-retary, so she switched off the pairing to allow his new secretary more time to focus on his work. It was an apt reply, but not an honest answer. Jill wondered out loud why she gave a damn if Harold approved of her decision, or not. After all, she was a name partner.

Harold played psychological games that some staff found difficult to handle. For instance, Harold sometimes created complex assignments with bogus deadlines and gave vague instructions to secretaries that were difficult to follow, but none of his secretar-ies called him on it. Instead, they struggled through tasks, contacting Harold repeatedly to confirm his instructions. Harold not only had an annoying habit of assigning complicated projects to secretaries with questionable instructions, but when these tasks were botched because of incoherent instructions, Harold would call other secretaries on his speakerphone and request additional assistance, explaining the assignment in an entirely different, more simplified manner.

Harold's dubious behavior appalled and befuddled many secretaries. He made most of them feel incompetent and incapable of following the simplest instructions. This was Harold's way of playing favorites among the office staff and keeping the environment competitive. But when Harold's daughter called him from her new job, sobbing because she had encountered similar tactics at *her* workplace, Harold sought to sober Jessica up with firm words. He urged her to get back to work. Perhaps, Harold recognized his own behavior on Jessica's accusations about her new boss.

Meanwhile, working with Harold was dispiriting. He frequently left a pitcher he used to water his plants dripping wet on my desk ledge, asking me to return it to the kitchen. Then, he started demanding that I water his plants. I told Harold, *"Absolutely not!"* He became fiercely angry at my defiance, going from one extreme to another. We exchanged heated words. He made me want to reach for something sharp or go upside his head with a baseball bat.

Daily assignments became chores that I felt loathe to do. One day, Harold entered his office as I was in a stooped position searching through a pile of papers on the floor. When I stood up without reaching for anything to balance myself, he said, "That's impressive." His eyes searched me eagerly. I flattered him with a pained, pretentious smile.

The next day, Harold entered the office and instructed me to search for flights to New York. He planned to visit with a client there before attending a wedding in Portland. I searched for several flight options, and after narrowing his choices, Harold decided to leave for New York late Thursday afternoon to meet with his client the next day. Harold's last-minute decision to inform me of his travel plans sent my day into a tailspin since he insisted on sending out bills with signed correspondence to clients before his departure.

On Thursday morning, I arrived at the office earlier than usual. I browsed online news stories and read my horoscope for the day while eating a breakfast sandwich. At 8:30, I logged onto Outlook and checked my emails.

I logged into American Airlines' website to request early check-in for Harold and printed his boarding passes for travel to New York and Portland. After printing the boarding passes, I two-hole-punched the itinerary and boarding passes then placed the paperwork in a two-pronged travel folder. It was a requirement of Harold's. As the day progressed, I rushed about completing several tasks before Harold's departure. After a laborious day of tending to Harold's unending requests, I was happy to call a taxi to take him to the airport.

Pamela Fohshay, another attorney on my pairing, worked mostly behind the closed door of her office—that is, until she needed my assistance. In hasty, almost fitful tantrums, Pamela frequently emerged from her office complaining that her computer malfunctioned. However, when I attempted to assist her, Pamela was reluctant to allow me access to her computer. Rather than turn over her computer, Pamela preferred that I tell her how to make it work while she followed my instructions. It was irritating to work with Pamela. She was unappreciative, arrogant, and withheld gratitude whenever any assistance I gave resolved her problems. I could see that working with Pamela would be an ongoing, thankless endeavor.

To ease my frustration, Sonia, a paralegal who also worked with Pamela, admitted that Pamela was stubborn and rooted in her ways. Although Sonia's comment didn't necessarily fix the problem, it did alleviate some of the tension. But then again, I had witnessed both staff and attorneys flip-flop from allies to enemies. Sonia herself was not particularly pleasant, and her manner was generally sarcastic. Even the receptionist, Gina, was an oddball. She spent her entire lunch hour in a stall in the ladies' room watching TV talk show hosts. I didn't know what to make of the office staff. They were a tricky bunch. Yet, Priyal touted that the firm was one of the best places to work. I beg to differ.

At this point, I didn't know who to believe, much less trust. Work relationships at the office had gone wrong for so long that a dysfunctional atmosphere became the norm, no matter how hard Priyal tried to mask it with office happy hours and social events. And, when the office *did* appear calmer than usual, she used gossip to instigate more trouble. I noticed, too, that Priyal and others in the office tried not to address me by name. Instead, they walked up on me and started conversations without a greeting. One time a paralegal tried addressing me by saying, "Hey, you!" I quickly straightened that bitch out and let her know my name is NOT "hey you." I told her where I come from in DC, we call people by their names. Apparently, some staff had a problem with me being vocal about it and continued to annoy me. But like Mr. Kramer, I had a savvy ability to rise above it. So, staff became unfriendly and deceptive. They told Priyal that I was anti-social when in actuality, they excluded me from conversations by shutting down all communication when I showed up.

I observed a stern sadness that Sonia wore on her face while working at the office. It reflected the degree of negativity she had endured over the years, which Sonia felt compelled to regurgitate whenever a new employee joined the firm. I recalled Sonia's warning to "watch out" for Priyal on my first day at the office.

After a difficult work week, I decided to relax and unwind over the weekend and rest up for the following week since Harold would return to the office on Monday. My job was not work-life balanced, and I found working with Harold rather impinging.

By now, Harold must have been meeting with his client in New York, having the most expensive steak dinner on the menu, for which he would bring back receipts for me to reconcile. He had no idea of what was about to unfold.

The next morning, Harold awoke frenzied, rushing around to gather his belongings before the taxi arrived to take him to the airport for his flight to Portland. The taxi driver raced through New York City traffic to get Harold to the airport on time for his flight. When the taxi driver arrived at JFK Airport, Harold paid the fare, grabbed his briefcase and travel bag, and bolted into the airport to check-in.

The TSA agent scrutinized Harold's driver's license and boarding pass then cleared him for travel. It was not until Harold gathered his belongings from the airport security bins and tied his shoes that he looked more closely at his itinerary. To his dismay, I inadvertently booked Harold on a flight to Portland, Oregon, instead of Portland, Maine. Harold exploded in a fit of rage at the airport as he searched through his iPhone for my phone number, but to his astonishment, my contact information was no longer there. Harold called Priyal to report the snafu and to assist him with changing his itinerary.

Like a whirlwind, the weekend was over. Priyal arrived at work Monday morning and, to her surprise, found an envelope on the floor when she unlocked her office door. In it, she found my access card and timesheet. Perplexed, Priyal called me and inquired about the contents in the envelope. I told her I quit and abruptly rang off. I left Priyal in a lurch, saddled with the task of finding a new secretary. I didn't give two fucks about them. That was their mutha-fuckin' problem.

\* \* \*

I worked for three attorneys at O'Rourke & Fielding, LLP—Clifford, Lloyd and John—in their respective practice areas of bankruptcy, trademarks/copyrights and patent law. The bulk of my workflow came from Clifford, the bankruptcy partner.

I prepared and e-filed Chapter Eleven petitions using Bankruptcy Pro, drafted Proofs of Claim, Affidavits, Motions, Plans of Reorganization, and Disclosure Statements. In addition, I requested hearing transcripts and recordings of Section 341 meetings; monitored bankruptcy and adversary proceeding case dockets and provided Clifford with status updates; prepared Witness and Exhibit Lists for emergency hearings; drafted, formatted, finalized, and e-filed Fee Applications; e-filed Notices of Appearance, Applications to Employ, Retainer Distributions, and Monthly Operating Reports; arranged telephonic hearings with bankruptcy judges; prepared mailings for over one hundred creditors and interested parties; submitted conflicts checks for potential and existing clients; entered billable time, and made travel arrangements. One day, after I completed an assignment for Clifford, he expressed gratitude.

"Paige, I can't tell you what a relief it is to finally work with an assistant that understands bankruptcy law."

We worked well together in the beginning. But soon, Clifford began assigning me tasks well beyond the scope of my position. While I was not an attorney, the complexity of cram-downs required critical thinking skills. I told one secretary, "I'm working so hard, I'm getting dizzy."

I reviewed Chapter Eleven plans of reorganization to determine the cram-down status, which required the approval of at least one class of impaired creditors, excluding votes cast by corporate insiders. However, at the request of a proponent of the plan, the court could confirm the plan, so long as the plan was "fair and equitable." But additional criteria needed to meet cram-down standards included that secured creditors retain a lien on collateral or proceeds and receive deferred cash payments equal to the collateral or unsecured creditors had to be paid in full else no holder of junior claims could receive any payment, at least that's how I understood it according to the Bankruptcy Code. But just as I began making headway on this project, along came Annie.

Annie was a temp that Gayle, the firm administrator, had hired permanently. However, Annie had only worked at the firm for one month. And before that, she worked as a cashier at a grocery store. So, Annie didn't have the know-how or skill set to complete tasks assigned by her attorneys. Instead of taking notes when given instructions, Annie pretended she knew what she was doing. Not only had the firm paid a finder's fee for hiring Annie, but she also continued to be a liability.

Annie constantly interrupted my workday, re-asking the same questions. How to handle incoming mail? What were the procedures for filing documents electronically with courts? How to find client matter numbers assigned by the accounting department? There were instructions that the other legal secretaries and I'd given to Annie so many times prior, I'd lost count. Mostly all of the other secretaries stopped helping Annie, so I became her go-to person for getting assignments done.

One day, Annie showed up at my desk in a frantic panic asking for assistance with filing a document with the court. She claimed that none of the other legal secretaries would help her. I told Annie that it would be a good idea for her to take notes that she could refer back to instead of re-asking the same questions over and over again. But Annie continued working mindlessly, riding the coattail of my knowledge. Then, late one afternoon, a legal secretary showed up at my desk and handed me a post-it note. It said that Annie had just been fired. I suppose Gayle thought if Annie performed the functions often enough, she would eventually catch on. Unfortunately, the firm had invested seven months of payroll checks in Annie, but it never registered.

Aside from Clifford, I worked primarily in an administrative capacity for Lloyd and John and made occasional travel arrangements for Lloyd to partici- pate at speaking engagements. Once I got the hang of my bankruptcy workload with Clifford, I found something productive to do with a little extra time on my hands.

I pioneered a business development opportu- nity whereby I secured speaking engagements for Lloyd, which aligned with his trademark and copy- right practice. As a result, I landed a CLE webinar with the Montana Bar Association and a one-hour briefing seminar with Practising Law Institute that generated revenues in excess of one hundred seven- teen thousand dollars.

Lloyd excelled at speaking engagements on the subjects of blockchain and cybersecurity and acquired some new clients as a result. Lloyd was pleased with my "thinking outside of the box" to help him build his practice. Not everyone was happy, though.

Clifford directed some resentment towards me and began creating bogus emergency assignments to compete with any free time I would otherwise use to organize speaking engagements for Lloyd. For instance, Clifford would tell me that we had a fil- ing due that same day or create "emergency" assign- ments that required my immediate attention.

Clifford was bald, tall and dark. He was a mature man but looked good for his age, and he knew it. Clifford hated to be told that he was wrong about anything. And, if you were the accuser, you would have to hear him out—for however long—until he proved to you that he was right. Then, he would strut off in "George Jefferson fashion" after he got you told. I observed his behavior with other attorneys. But shit rolls downhill.

Blaming me must have been a hobby for Clifford because he did so regularly. When Clifford assigned tasks, he preferred to put documents in plastic folders. One day, he rushed out of his office asking me for his folders. When I told him I didn't have them, he said, "Stop what you're doing right now and find my folders." I walked into Clifford's office, looked around, and found some folders under a stack of papers. Ever since I started arranging speaking engagements for Lloyd, Clifford tried to find the right button to push to send me over the edge.

Around Christmastime, Clifford came into the office and told me that he forgot my gift in his car. He mentioned it on and off again that day to remind me that I needed to get my gift from him before he left for the holidays.

Near the end of the day, Clifford left the office. I received a call from him asking me to meet him downstairs at his car to pick up my gift. The box was small. When I got home, I opened the box and found a bracelet. It was too small, almost childlike. So, I re-boxed the bracelet, placed it in one of my high-end shopping bags, and left it atop his desk with a note that read, "I appreciate the gift bracelet. However, it was too tight to fit. By the way, I only accept gifts from Neiman's."

Clifford was livid!

To get back at me, he deliberately interfered with my business development project with Lloyd by creating a last-minute, full-court press each month to get his billable time entries done. In fact, he assigned me the arduous task of going through his emails line by line in search of his billable time. *This was maddening!*

Clifford called me at home some evenings and weekends requesting his logins and passwords to file documents with bankruptcy courts. When I told him I didn't bring that information home with me, he demanded that I do so because he may call me for it in the future. However, Clifford fought hard against approving any overtime for accepting his calls during non-working hours.

I warned Clifford about the DC Bitch in me when he started finger-pointing aggressively at my face. When I sent an email to my group of attorneys about my plans to take a vacation, Clifford came out of his office and confronted me about it. "You should have requested *permission* to take a vacation!" he yelled. He walked away in inextinguishable anger.

Clifford's mood fluctuated like an untimely tide. He had a tendency to slap labels on people. And once he did, he was pretty much convinced. But that was just his beliefs working in opposition to others'. He judged so critically. And, of course, he was *always* right. So, I let him be until he accused me of someone else's error.

One day, after stewing in his anger, Clifford came out of his corner office embroiled in an obvious rage. He approached my workstation demanding to know why a pleading had been filed incorrectly four times on the bankruptcy court docket. Even though I reminded Clifford that I was out of the office on vacation at the time the pleading was filed and that Virginia, a litigation secretary, had apologized to me earlier that morning for misfiling the pleading, he would hear none of it.

To make matters worse, Clifford stood towering above me, his nostrils flaring. He yelled at me and pointed his finger at my face accusingly, "You are not going to blame Virginia for this!"

I yelled back, "And you are not going to blame me for it when I was on vacation!"

"You are not following my instructions!" Clifford said through clenched teeth. I could tell from his demeanor that he wanted to put his hands on me in a bad way. I challenged him with choice words.

"Your instructions are convoluted!" I said.

"Your thoughts are convoluted!" he snapped back.

*Oh, we went at each other!* Ego to ego. I figured the force was with me since I had not invited any of this bullshit nonsense. So, I stood up and grabbed the closest object on my desk to defend myself then clobbered him on the head with a Swingline two-hole punch. "Get out of my face!" I yelled. At that moment, another secretary walked up and asked, "What's going on?"

"I hit my head on the cabinet above Paige's desk, Clifford told the secretary. We both knew he lied. Then, Clifford made a beeline out of my work area.

At the beginning of our work relationship, Clifford had said to me, "Paige, I can't tell you what a relief it is to finally work with an assistant that understands the bankruptcy practice. My last assistant just didn't have the head for this business." But since that time, something had gone awry. Clifford started arguments with me over the minutest things. For instance, when I told him I was taking vacation, he would go off wildly, railing about it. One time, I responded to an email that Clifford sent to me strongly suggesting that I ask permission next time. I told him, "I'm a G.A.W. (grown-ass woman) and suggested he get out of parental-mode. Clifford called me into his office. He admonished me in a hushed tone. His unpleasant words oozed with volcanic anger.

"Paige," he said, "you're heading down a very wrong path!"

"Based on what?" I asked. Tongue-tied, Clifford exhaled in exasperation and turned to face his computer. It was his way of dismissing me from his office. Before leaving his office, I said to him, "One minute you're praising me for a job well done; the next, you're throwing me under the bus for someone else's mistake! Make up your mind! Indecisive motherfucker! And by the way, if you're looking for an argument, write an MSJ." He turned around and stretched his eyes at me, shocked by my audacity. I would not allow myself to be jerked around by his private whims and fancies.

But what was *really* eating at Clifford was he had heard through the grapevine about my carousing and rendezvous with his client Vernon Seymour. The last time Vernon visited Dallas for a business meeting, I met him that evening at a glamorous restaurant downtown at the hotel where he stayed. Clifford threatened to report me to Human Resources for having relations with his client. I laughed in his face and egged him on, "Go ahead!" I urged him. "But just so you know, I own my own pussy." When I returned to my desk, Boz Scaggs' "Lowdown" was playing on my desk radio...

> Nothin' you can't handle
> Nothin' you ain't got
> Put your money on the table
> And drive it off the lot
> Turn on that old love light
> And turn a "maybe" to a "yes"
> Same old schoolboy game got you into this mess

\* \* \*

Later that afternoon, Clifford came out of his office. He was much calmer now. "Paige," he said, "I'm leaving to fly to Houston for the emergency hearing tomorrow." I didn't respond, so he repeated himself. "Clifford," I said, I can help you get out of here, but it won't be pretty." He quickly disappeared.

Surprisingly, my very volatile work relationship with Clifford wasn't the terminating factor that ended my employment with O'Rourke & Fielding, LLP. It was a singular revolt—a stance—of my very vocal decision not to participate in an elementary event in celebration of staff for Administrative Professional's Day. An email invite, which included cartoon animals, was sent to staff announcing a trip to the Dallas Zoo. It was an affront not only to me but also to my ruling planet Uranus. I gave them a piece of my mind. *I'll be damned if...!*

For all my hard work and effort drafting bankruptcy petitions, fee applications, notices of retainers, and motions, all of which required certificate of service mailings to over a hundred interested parties, not to mention a barrage of administrative tasks, including last minute end-of-the-month time entries that required sacrificing *my* lunch hour to enter an entire month of billable time for two procrastinating attorneys before close of business in a single day... *Whew!* While this was how business got done and we managed to pull it off month after month for the past two years, I was not about to let O'Rourke & Fielding skimp on rewarding my relentless diligence. And

I said as much when I clicked the "Reply All" button sending my email to staff as well as Gayle.

In so many words, I told all of them that the email inviting staff to the zoo for Administrative Professionals Day was not an event worthy of my attendance, nor did it meet my customary standards for such an occasion. I was accustomed to receiving lavish gifts from DC attorneys like three-hundred-dollar Visa gift cards, Perrier Jouët Grand Brut (champagne glasses included), lunches at upscale restaurants like Proof, and annual subscriptions to *The New Yorker* magazine. For good measure, I threw in an advertisement of a nine-hundred-dollar Lois Hill bracelet in my reply email. I was surprised by the outpouring of support I received from co-workers, some of whom rarely spoke to me. They congratulated me with celebratory high-fives, confiding that they too felt the same as I did about the email invite, but for fear of consequences, they decided to go along to get along. *Not me!*

About two weeks later, while I was preparing a certificate of service mailing for a motion I had just filed electronically, Gayle interrupted me in the copy room at 4:15 pm. She asked me to report to a conference room. When I arrived, Stan, one of the attorneys at the firm, was already seated. Gayle asked me to take a seat at the head of the conference room table. After I sat down, she informed me that my employment with the firm was terminated effective immediately. Without flinching, I responded buoyantly,

"Okay." My cheerful outlook, considering the circumstances, caught Gayle off guard. After informing me of the firm's termination policy, Gayle handed me my final paycheck, walked with me to my desk to gather my belongings, then escorted me to the lobby. When I entered the elevator to leave the firm for the last time, Gayle said, in a seething, obnoxious tone, "Good luck." Honestly, it was a relief to finally be out of O'Rourke & Fielding for good. Apparently, Dave Chappelle was right, "keeping it real" could go wrong. Except, I knew how to *keep it real cute*. A month to the day later, I was working up the street at another law firm in downtown Dallas.

# CHAPTER NINE

## Wait... You Lied to Me!

"For any system to function well, it needs to be integrated and coherent with all its components or contributing elements relating and working well together."

~David Spangler

*After a couple of hours, I merged onto US-395N via exit 188 toward Hermiston, Stanfield and Umatilla. I drove an hour and a half longer, then turned left on Columbia River Highway to US-730W. By now, it was early afternoon. I stopped at a Wal-Mart to take a break from the road. I bought a sandwich and a gallon of water.*

*It turned out to be a very warm day. I changed out of the cabled sweater I was wearing and into a short-sleeved cotton shirt. I got back on the road and merged onto I-82W toward Kennewick and Yakima crossing into Washington.*

*I made it to Seattle around 4:30 pm. By now, it was raining. I decided to drive downtown. It was HILLACIOUS! After a succession of turns, I found myself on Spring Street—one of the highest hills. The stoplight caught me. DAMN! I was tilted back, waiting for the light to change. When it did, too afraid to let go of the brake to press the gas pedal, I held the brake with both feet, then pressed the gas pedal as I eased off the brake. My car skidded, jolting forward. I turned right and headed toward I-5, not knowing exactly where I was going—just away from downtown. I ended up staying at a hotel in Bellevue.*

* * *

My carousel work experiences, up to now, had its highs and lows, which resembled a series of soap-opera-like scenarios: *As the Work Turns*, *Work Life to Live*, *All My Work* and *The Work and The Restless.*

In my latest role as Litigation Legal Secretary at Dulaney & Crenshaw, PLLC, I supported a partner and two associates in the firm's employment and labor law practice group. I was deluged with litigation cases all day long that ranged anywhere from slip and falls to hair salon brawls to EEOC complaints involving discriminations and wrongful terminations to insurance claims related to break-ins and theft of personal property. There was no lack of work, that's for sure.

My job consisted primarily of requesting conflicts checks for new and existing client matters related mostly to litigation and discrimination cases, filing notices of removals, contacting claims adjusters to obtain insurance policy information to enter in a billing database, and calendaring response deadlines to complaints, petitions, discovery, initial analysis reports, and mediations.

Upon immediate acceptance of new litigation cases, I drafted engagement and litigation hold letters for attorney review, approval and signature to forward to clients, meticulously proofread initial analysis reports, which required several rounds of revisions before finalizing and forwarding an original signed report to clients, created draft shells for attorneys to respond to Requests for Admissions, Requests for Disclosure, Requests for Production and Objections and Requests for Interrogatories, prepared demand letters to forward to opposing counsel, drafted settlement agreements following successful mediation, drafted correspondence letters enclosing settlement checks to opposing counsel, reviewed insurance litigation guideline procedures related to reporting, strategy, budgeting, and billing requirements, prepared notebooks for pleadings, discovery, mediation, and trial, approved deposition invoices for payment, and prepared expense reimbursements for attorneys.

The work kept all involved jumping hurdles to meet deadlines and, if one was missed, staff were quick to pass the blame. Hi-jinks was the game. Not many staff knew each other too well. Most of us were new hires. We wondered about that, but there was little time for idle contemplation. So, I tended to focus on the work. As litigation legal secretary, it was also my responsibility to maintain and update electronic calendaring for my attorneys' case deadlines. The majority of my time was spent tracking and completing assignments. Then, on to the next. As a result of the inability, unwillingness or incompetence of other staff, responsibility for work that wasn't even *my* responsibility got shifted onto my workload. Some staff acted as if their work wasn't theirs to do. Mental adeptness was clearly lacking here. So, without shirking the work, I drafted fifteen shells for responses to discovery requests in a single day. Even though this was part of the job—other duties as assigned— no one bothered to say, *thank you.* To further complicate an already malicious work environment, I learned that a paralegal tried to take credit for some discovery responses I previously drafted, assigning me a task to "review and finalize discovery responses" *she* claimed she initially drafted. I got her privy to my email-chain-game by letting her know that I had originally drafted those discovery responses. "No, you will not take improper ownership of work that I produced!" She backed down.

Since there had been a high degree of turnover in my position—four litigation assistants in the past two years—Maxine, a partner attorney for whom I was hired to work, had little interaction with me, at first. She preferred to flow her work instructions to me through her paralegal, Ivy. During the first few weeks of my employment at Dulaney & Crenshaw, Ivy assigned, or rather, saddled me with the redundant task of preparing coversheets and spines for numerous notebooks for pleadings, discovery, mediations and case timelines. After completing about fifty or more notebooks, Ivy gave me more substantive assignments that involved contacting legal services vendors to arrange for court reporters and videographers to take depositions. After using Ivy as her intermediary to see how things would work out between us, Maxine finally came around, accepted me as her assistant, and put me in charge of managing her mediation calendar. Maxine also entrusted me with the meticulous task of proofreading initial analysis reports that, upon her final review, were sent to clients. Before I knew it, we had established a great work relationship. Then, during a casual conversation with Ivy, she asked me, "Do you masturbate?"

I was not completely shocked by Ivy's curiosity about me. It was typical in my normal day-to-day. Besides, it wasn't the first time a woman had taken an interest in me. There had been others. While working in DC, I frequently lunched with Amber, a co-worker.

Amber was of mixed ethnicity—a combination of African, German and Indian heritage. She was attractive. Amber always wore her hair a straight shoulder-length with a part down the middle. It suited her oval-shaped face. Anyway, Amber was the type of woman that other legal secretaries at the firm admired. She kept to herself, minded her own business, and did her work. After befriending Amber, she shared a little bit of her personal history with me. Some of the other legal secretaries, who saw me going to lunch with Amber, asked me about her. They wanted to know what she was like. I told them, "Amber is an Aquarius, like me." And that's all they needed to know.

When the weather turned cold, Amber and I didn't go out for lunch as much anymore. Sometimes, Amber drove us to a designated restaurant in her plush Range Rover to pick up lunch. After a few trips of picking up our lunch, Amber suggested we eat lunch in a private file room at the office. During our lunch conversations, Amber opened up to me. She had married her high school sweetheart, had two kids and recently began entertaining the idea of exploring something new and different. I wasn't exactly sure what Amber meant by "exploring something new and different," but I soon found out.

One day, after I put a frozen meal into the microwave for lunch, I proceeded down the hall. I heard someone—a woman's voice—call out my name softly. So softly, in fact, that when I turned around and saw Amber somehow, by osmosis, I knew exactly what she meant when she said she wanted to explore something new and different. Amber asked me to have lunch with her in "our little room." I agreed. A short while later, I met her in the file room.

While eating lunch, Amber asked if she could see my pussy. She said, "I want to know if it looks like how I imagine it—pretty and pink inside." Confidently, I scooted up to the edge of my chair, leaned back, put one leg up on the table, and pulled my panties aside, letting her look at my pretty pussy. The next thing I knew, Amber was in front of me on her knees, thrusting her tongue inside of me. I watched her taste my pussy for the first time. Her nose pressed up against my clitoris. I relished the erotic pleasure lavished on me, as Amber tongued me vigorously. I got so wet! She licked and gulped and swallowed. I had no idea Amber intended to go down on me like that! WOW!!! She practically feasted on my pussy!

But Ivy, a native Texan, was a different story. She was the butchy-type, and when she got angry, *which was often*, she became almost impossible to cope with. Ivy frequently mouthed off irately at staff in the office. She was rowdy. I'm not sure how or why she took to me because I tried my best to keep my distance from her, but working for Maxine linked us together.

Just when working with Ivy was beginning to feel tortuous, she unexpectedly turned in her resignation. Like most of the staff, I was relieved. Ivy's last day was the same as the firm's holiday party, but to avoid any risk of Ivy showing up, Maxine asked Ivy not to attend. Little did I know, this day would be a significant turning point for me, too.

A month prior, I interviewed with Engrid, a recruiter, for a bankruptcy paralegal position at a law firm up the street from Dulaney & Crenshaw. Engrid had called, asking if I was available to interview with the firm administrator. We arranged a meeting for the following day. I was invited back to the firm two days later to interview with the attorneys. The next day, Engrid called me with an offer. I accepted.

On the morning of the firm's holiday party, Marisol Hernandez, the Office Manager at Dulaney & Crenshaw, handed me an envelope and said, "Merry Christmas!" I thanked her. We had a brief conversation. Then, Marisol went her way. After about an hour, I opened the envelope, which was a holiday card from the firm wishing me "Happy Holidays."

It's a typical policy, at most law firms, for employees to receive holiday bonuses by mid-December. Moreover, my offer letter stated that I would receive a holiday bonus. Maxine told me about a week ago that she intended to cushion the firm's bonus with a gift of her own since the firm really didn't give that much of a bonus to staff. So, I let it ride—for a while—and gave Marisol the benefit of the doubt. Maybe she was waiting until the holiday party to distribute holiday bonuses to employees, I surmised.

Nothing fancy. It was a catered party—buffet style. I chatted with staff and attorneys sitting at the table with me. Trivia games were played, prizes won, and after a while, the party started to wind down. I got a sneaking feeling that Marisol wouldn't be handing out holiday bonuses after all. So, when I saw Marisol going back to the buffet for dessert, I asked her about my bonus. "Oh," she said nonchalantly, "You won't get a bonus until the end of *next* year." Somewhat bemused, I said, "Oh, okay." I guess she showed *me* who was boss.

*Wait a minute, bitch!* Rewind that back like a transcription tape!! *Wait!... WHAT? YOU LIED TO ME IN MY OFFER LETTER!* This Pinocchio-bitch tried to play me! I'm a person, not a puppet. Revenge yanked on a string of thoughts in my mind. I'd show this bitch a thing or two about fucking with *me!*

Later that afternoon, I saw Marisol strutting around the office like a confident ostrich.

I played it cool. "One trick at a time," I reminded myself. This bitch had no idea I had reshuffled the deck and was holding the Ace of Spades. I kept my head down and continued working cooperatively with everyone.

The next day, I drafted an email to Marisol expressing my confusion about not receiving a holiday bonus when my offer letter stated that I would. And the fact that I recently received an impressive evaluation from each of my attorneys, I asked Marisol if there was anything I needed to improve to ensure that I would receive a holiday bonus at the end of *next* year. I copied my attorneys on the email then sent it to Marisol.

Unexpectedly, Maxine bolted from her office, ran into Marisol's office, and slammed the door shut. She pelted Marisol with angry words. Maxine demanded Marisol tell her why she had withheld my holiday bonus. It took some grilling from Maxine before Marisol finally admitted that *she* single-handedly decided to withhold my holiday bonus. After a severe scolding from Maxine, Marisol put in a last-minute check request for my holiday bonus. To save face, she initiated the request the following morning telling me, "You will, in fact, receive a holiday bonus of three hundred eighty dollars, before taxes."

Mind you, I was accustomed to receiving three-thousand-dollar bonuses, not working for peanuts. So, when Maxine walked breezily by my desk and handed me a thickly padded envelope as she cheerfully said, "Merry Christmas," I figured there would be something in it to buoy me up. Surely Maxine understood my added value to her team. I had assisted her with obtaining collections payments from clients that brought in cash receipts of well over one hundred twenty thousand dollars. So, I opened the envelope from Maxine and looked inside. There was a $100 Target gift card and one hundred dollars in cash.

I put the cash and gift card in my purse and continued working as if I would continue. Daily, I added to the already elaborate display of holiday cards from clients at my workstation, attended staff meetings and participated in brainstorming sessions. I even cozied up with Maxine and her group of attorneys at a holiday lunch. Since there were no more outstanding invoices due, Maxine was delighted. She relaxed, as she should, and started taking extended lunches. Meetings were held, changes were made, and I was told by Marisol that my attorney pairing would change.

All along, I had said administrative tasks stemming from work that partner attorneys assigned to associate attorneys should be handled by that associate attorney's legal secretary. But some of the associate's legal secretaries were considered junior secretaries, or, in my opinion, not qualified to do the work, as they looked for other more qualified secretaries to hand their work off to. Coattail riders—that's what I called them. I'd be damned if I would do my work and theirs, too! But, as I said, changes were made.

My suggestion with regard to work assigned to associate attorneys would now be implemented, in full force, effective in the coming new year. With that, two associate attorneys were also added to Maxine's group, which meant I would be responsible for *all* work Maxine generated and assigned to the two associate attorneys as well. NO THANK YOU! If Marisol thought she had pulled a fast one on me, I had a *real* surprise in store for these jokers.

On New Years' Day, I arrived at the office at 8:00 am, completed and signed my timesheet, placed it on my desk atop the firm's policy manual, and set my out-of-office email to send out the following auto-reply message the following day at 8:00 am:

> Paige Turner is no longer with the firm. If you need immediate assistance, please contact the Office Administrator, Marisol Hernandez.

I included Marisol's contact information in the email. I ghosted them.

# CHAPTER TEN

## Creative Gal vs. Company Girls et al.

> "Those of us who have made something of
> our lives will always look at those who haven't
> and see nothing but clowns."
>
> ~Thomas Wayne (Brett Cullen), *Joker* (2019)[2]

After work one evening, Bonita called me. She told me that she saw Reggie and he asked about me.

"I hope you don't mind. I told him you moved to Seattle," Bonita said.

I didn't mind, but after speaking with Bonita, I took some time to make a journal entry:

\* \* \*

*My first mistake was being too trusting in a place where double-dealing runs deep. I should have known better. Every day on my way to work, I saw the streets strewn with broken people whose dream it was to be nobody in particular but themselves. That obviously didn't work! Here, one needs to have the spirit of an Olympic champion to survive and thrive. No time for tears or feeling sorry for yourself will appeal to anyone. And don't even think of throwing yourself a pity party. Invitations will go unanswered! In fact, such sulking is frowned upon by some people—the ones actually trying to get someplace—bustling by the defeated ones wallowing in their trampled aspirations. You must endeavor to get somewhere in life (wherever that is) and make a name for yourself because it's not enough to just be yourself. You must be SOMEBODY! Who that SOMEBODY is, depends on you. But don't lose yourself in somebody else's definition of the SOMEBODY you ought to be or become! In the words of a wise man: "Don't accept criticism from anyone you wouldn't take advice from." In my own words, know who you are and what you stand for in this life because people will do more than try to hit you and run—they will try to stomp on you! Yes! Life can be like that! But when you get good at living life, it flows, and good things flow to you. No one can alter your destiny when you've got good karma.*

*You won't find me regretting a life of bankrupt dreams! What you will find is someone that has the clarity and resilience to realize her dreams. Only I can make my dreams come true.*

\* \* \*

146

Like Dorothy from Kansas, I had made it to *Emerald City*, but there was no "Yellow Brick Road" here. Instead, Seattle was overrun with homelessness. I saw tent cities (makeshift shelters) in plain view along I-405 as the 212 express bus traveled from Bellevue to downtown Seattle. It was an eyesore. There were tents lined up on both sides of the street under the viaduct. The homeless took shelter wherever they could find it. Upon exiting Westlake station one rainy morning, I observed a homeless woman standing frozen-like in the cold, holding an open box of cereal with both hands while she stared straight ahead, slightly upward. In fact, on my way to work, I was stepping over homeless people sleeping on the sidewalks wrapped in blankets. It was cold.

On my way home from work, as the 212 Eastgate Factoria express bus made its way down Second Avenue, I saw homeless people sitting, sleeping and sprawled on the sidewalks near Pioneer Square. Others sat inside tents peering out. It was an atrocity to see people living at such poverty-stricken, debased levels that they couldn't even bathe, eat or sleep in proper living quarters on a daily basis. It was a dirty state of affairs.

When I arrived home after work one evening, I turned on the TV and Tucker Carlson's show featured Seattle in a segment called "Homeless in America." Since the airing of this segment, some progress has been made. The tents were removed from under the viaduct, and now there aren't as many homeless people sleeping downtown or on the sidewalks, but a large homeless population still remains in Seattle. According to some of the locals, legislation is slow here, so not much has been done.

After working about two months at Strobeck Keller LLP, an otherwise pleasant work environment, became fraught with tension. However, it wasn't a surprise. Camilla, a Legal Assistant, who resigned while on vacation, had warned me that Strobeck Keller was about to enter into a bad merger-marriage with Byers & Lowry LLC, another law firm. Camilla was a tenured Legal Assistant, who had worked at Strobeck Keller for more than twenty years. As I understood it, she didn't want to be around for the fallout. According to Camilla, the merger wasn't a mutual decision. Both firms needed each other financially in order to stay afloat.

Before leaving Strobeck Keller, Camilla pulled me aside. She told me that I would encounter problems at this office because I was a girlie-girl. "Most of the women in Seattle," said Camilla, "wear leggings, hoodies and other rugged outdoor gear to work. They don't dress very feminine, like you," she said. "I *had* noticed their attire," I told Camilla. I couldn't believe that some of these Company Girls et al. wore outdoorsy gear, which I considered too casual to wear in a professional environment. Some of these Company Girls dressed like they worked on a farm or in a warehouse. And the nerve of one of the Company Girls to suggest that I was showing too much skin by asking,

"Are you wearing pantyhose with that skirt?" "No," I replied. "My thighs are taut. I don't have cellulite." Lowering her spectacles halfway to peer at my naked legs, Dolores responded snidely, "Oh, you're lucky."

Camilla also told me that she made a note about me in her journal the first day we met.

"You are a very attractive, exotic-looking woman," Camilla said. "I admire you for being outgoing and adventurous, moving to the Pacific Northwest and all. But," Camilla urged me, "find employment elsewhere and leave Strobeck Keller."

To expedite my employment search, Camilla referred me to a recruiter who had recently placed her in a position that paid six thousand dollars more than her current salary.

Over the next few months, I learned that many of the Company Girls at Strobeck Keller had insecurity issues as well as manipulative agendas. So, I steered clear of them.

At the outset, some of the Company Girls were friendly. They complimented me on my appearance and were all up in my personal space like a dude trying to date me, especially when I wore clothing accenting my curves and slightly prominent derrière. These Company Girls didn't make a secret of sizing me up or walking behind me to get a rear view of my assets. One of the Company Girls, Lillian, asked me, "What is your secret to looking so good?"

"I don't try too hard," I told Lillian. "I simply wear stylish clothes that fit my personality." I wore professional business attire that showed off my puckered ass, embellished my outfits with belts that cinched my waistline, and sashayed around the office wearing high heels.

"I used to dress cute like you before I got married and had children," Lillian told me. "But pregnancy was unkind to me." Lillian gestured at her protruded belly. She was self-conscious about wearing clingy clothing to avoid attracting attention to a part of her body that she disliked. So, Lillian wore loose, matronly clothing that hung on her like a curtain. "Besides," Lillian continued, "I don't have the time to dress up and wear make-up anymore. I take care of my mother, who suffers with bouts of dementia."

One mid-June morning, I walked by Lillian's desk and said, "Good morning," in a cheery tone. She snapped back at me, "No! It's not a good morning."

"What's wrong?" I asked.

Lillian told me that her mother had another memory lapse last night. She tossed their kitten across the living room, mistaking it for a pillow. Lillian looked exhausted as she was now on her second cup of coffee. But Lillian was notorious for bringing her family drama to the office as well as finding things to complain about. She also brought her kids to the office, which I didn't understand since she told me her daughter, Elissa, had failed twelfth grade.

"Shouldn't Elissa be in summer school?" I asked Lillian.

Lillian said, "She's too far behind to catch up in summer school."

These Company Girls wanted to know all about my personal business. They bombarded me with questions like: "Are you married?" "Do you have any children?" "Do you know anyone in Seattle?" To which I responded, "No, no and no." Apparently, because I look like *I Woke Up Like This,* these bitch-ass Company Girls were hell-bent on finding something on me to satisfy their furious curiosity. Even some of the attorneys chimed in adding their two cents to the jealous ruckus. During their conversations, the Company Girls et al. whispered and snickered. Their intent was to laugh me to scorn. Meanwhile, I remained focused, because none of the Company Girls et al. were worth losing my composure over. Many of them bragged about their spouses and their families. Yet, I was their constant focal point. They prowled around my desk like jungle predators, which gave the impression that they weren't living so happily ever after, after all.

Now, the bizarre thing was, most of these Company Girls—bitch-boys included— tried to shame me by using anonymous email to antagonize me about problems that they grappled with—issues such as man-boobs, being overweight, loneliness, debt, thinning hair, belly-fat, cheating spouses, uncertainty about their future, and self-doubt. The Company Girls et al. were either obsessed with me or mindlessly bored. They went through the trouble to research my personal background information.

When the Company Girls discovered that my credit was less than satisfactory, they took to anonymous email to let me know they had found out about it. They harangued and berated me via anonymous email about my financial situation. I found the utter subterfuge undertaken to try to shame or intimidate me rather appalling. Why anyone would want to unnecessarily concern themselves with someone else's personal financial situation just for the sake of knowing, was beyond me. But I was armor-plated with an inner self-assurance that these Company Girls et al. couldn't figure out, much less, tamper with.

The Company Girls et al. tried to kick down the door of my dignity, shatter my confidence, attack my personhood; as if to defy my capability of becoming a writer and escape this workaday life? They inflated their self-importance, discussed tasks ostentatiously. They became territorially challenging. Almost everywhere I went, there they were trying to limit the scope of my boundaries within the office. The Company Girls et al. tried to make me feel like an outcast. But I was Edward Earl's granddaughter. And, I had his genetic dignity trait. Yes, the Company Girls tried to bully me, but I faced them head-on like two-way traffic on 287N—unflinchingly. What they hadn't realized is that I'd *already* become SOMEBODY. I wasn't searching for approval. Some years ago, I learned a valuable lesson: Never let anyone make you feel ashamed of yourself. *That is soul murder!*

In the meantime, I kept my foot on the gas pedal of my own life and continued writing this book, while listening to *Keep On* on the radio at my desk.

Monetarily speaking, I *was* living upside down. I had more financial liabilities than assets. *But who, in working-class America, doesn't? Why do you think I'm writing this book?* First, because I can. Second, to show ALL those *bitch-ass* bitches that I could maintain my focus and achieve my dream of becoming a writer. After all, I didn't white-knuckle drive through Teton territory, parts unknown, and beyond to the Pacific Northwest for nothing. I acquired something along the way—the courage to make my own dreams come true.

I was an enigma to those Company Girls et al. They couldn't figure me out. I'm a Creative Gal, but the Company Girls et al. envied my creativity and tried to do everything within their power to convert me to their Company Girl-clique. By comparison, they bolstered and praised their peers—so-called "model employees"—in an attempt to provide me with examples to follow. I rebuffed. *No thanks, bitches!* I wasn't auditioning to become the poster-employee for this firm. I wasn't interested in living a plain, unfulfilled, ordinary life. There was nothing about them to inspire me to emulate. I was simply looking for a safe workspace that embraced creativity and welcomed the birth of my writer-muse.

What these Company Girls et al. might find surprising is, I've been an Aquarius my entire life. Uranus *will* push the boundaries, as I have faced down many odds. These Company Girls et al. were just another one of them. I'd developed, practiced, and now successfully applied the art of David Foster Wallace's definition of "true freedom."[3] I had become conscious and aware enough to choose what I paid attention to and how I construct meaning from experience.

I was hired by this firm to work as a floater legal assistant, but when a paralegal/project manager opening became available, Lynn Beckett, the Human Resources Manager, offered me the position.

A short while after I began working in my new role as the paralegal/project manager, the Company Girls et al. became enraged with jealousy. They launched a vilifying attack on me via anonymous email because they were angry that I'd been promoted to a paralegal position having worked only two months at Strobeck Keller. Most of these Company Girls had been legal assistants for ten years or more and were content doing just that. They tried everything they could to distract me from working. They frequently paraded past my desk, asked useless questions that had no relevance whatsoever to my work, and stalked me in the office. One of them followed me into the bathroom and peeped in the stall while I was inside.

To my surprise, in the following weeks, my workload diminished significantly. It was an attempt to deflate my ambition with boredom and offset the culminating mood-swings of the Company Girls et al. I didn't understand why they were so angry and up in arms about my recent promotion, considering most of them knew that I'd worked previously in the same capacity as a bankruptcy paralegal in Denver and Dallas. But if they had a problem with my ambition, that was their dilemma to sort out.

I had more than "a pocket full of dreams." *I had big plans!* I intended to finish writing my book, which I progressively worked on before 8:30 am and after 5:00 pm at the office since I didn't have a computer at home. I arrived at the office as early as 6:00 am and left as late as 7:00 pm to give myself time to type up my story during non-working hours.

Soon, my early arrivals and late departures attracted the attention of the Company Girls et al. I could tell that someone had accessed my computer remotely. I heard their commentary, gasps and hisses from nearby workstations as they read my story verbatim as I typed it. They became a barometer for my story. *They were intrigued!* Like some previously long-time friends with whom I shared the first few chapters. They went off the barometer rails, so to speak. *It was too much for them!* But this book was never about making friends. It was about making money; as almost everything I did, writing this book was pretty much a transaction. I'd read *Life Is Long If You Know How To Use It*. So, I didn't give them the time of day, or the satisfaction of reading the remaining chapters of my book. I stopped working on my book during non-work hours at the office. Instead, I finished it at the local library.

Turns out, I'm not a fellatio-master porn star after all. *I'm a mutha-fuckin' bestselling author!* And that was something the Company Girls et al. couldn't compete with—*my dreams!* By now, they understood that I was not at this firm for the long haul, but the short-term. I was a come-from-behind, win-at-all-costs dark horse willing to do whatever it takes. *And I was winning!*

Finally, I played my Ace of Spades. On August 29, 2019, I turned in my two weeks' notice:

> My last day will be Friday, September 13th. I'm embarking on a writer career.
>
> As stipulated in my offer letter attached hereto, I will repay the firm's two-thousand-dollar bonus, as my employment with the firm was short-term (April 22, 2019–September 13, 2019). Thank you for the opportunity.
>
> Kind regards,
> Paige Turner

After that, I turned up the volume a little on my desk radio when I heard "Ain't No Stoppin' Us Now." If those Company Girls et al. mistook me for granite, thought I'd go, "Abracadabra, leave and come back?" *I'd show them! I'm a different kind of diamond!* As I said, I wasn't interested in inching my way up the salary scale with incremental increases, climbing the corporate ladder, or breaking a glass ceiling. I'd carved out a career for myself as a writer. And *poof!* Just like that, the office reverted to boredom.

The next day, I went to Mel's Market for lunch. On my way back to the office, I saw a deranged, mangy-looking homeless man in front of the building throwing a screwdriver up in the air and letting the chips fall where they may, so to speak. I KNOW ONE MUTHAFUCKIN THING! I thought. DON'T GET FUCKED UP OUT HERE! *Exactly...twirl that bitch one time and make it disappear...since he wanna be a damn magician!* That's some shit my bestie Roxanne said later when I told her about it. But looking at this homeless man at closer range after crossing the street, I supposed, we all have a bit of leashed craziness in us that needs to come out. *But whatever! He better fold that shit up and put it in his pocket.*

After work, I went to Pike Place Market to get some Dungeness crabs. It was jam-packed with people. I got two Dungeness crabs and asked to have them cleaned since I didn't know how to do it.

When my crabs were ready, a guy at the seafood counter called my number and told me the price. As I reached for my purse, a gentleman behind me with a very commanding voice said, "I'm paying for the lady." His voice awakened a surge of dormant emotions. I turned around. *It was Reggie!*

# Endnotes

1      Sherry Argov, *Why Men Marry Bitches* (2011).

2      Anthony Lane, "Todd Phillips's 'Joker' Is No Laughing Matter," *The New Yorker* (September 27, 2019).

3      D. T. Max, "David Foster Wallace's struggle to surpass 'Infinite Jest,'" *The New Yorker* (February 28, 2009).

## About the Author

Pear Yonsei is a native of Washington DC, who now resides in the Pacific Northwest. Pear is a graduate of the University of Maryland at College Park, where she studied History with a focus in African Studies and earned a Bachelor of Arts degree. In her spare time, Pear enjoys listening to good music, eating blue crabs while carousing with friends, and reading about astrology from trusted sources. During winter she becomes reclusive and likes to reflect on her own profound thoughts as well as those of the great writers. Pear appreciates the other-worldly beauty of exotic destinations, and hopes to soon visit Morocco and The French Riviera.